Chautauqua After Hours

Stephane
best Mary Keating

by
Mary Keating

Deer Run Press
Cushing, Maine

Copyright © 2019 Mary Keating

All rights reserved. No part this book may be reproduced or transmitted in any form or by any means, electronic or mechanical, including photo-copying, recording, or by any information storage and retrieval system, without written permission from the copyright owner.

This is a work of fiction. Names, characters, places and incidents either are the product of the author's imagination or are used fictitiously, and any resemblance to any actual persons (living or dead), events, or locales is entirely coincidental.

Library of Congress Card Number: 2019937409

ISBN: 978-1-937869-10-6

First Printing, 2019

Published by
Deer Run Press
8 Cushing Road
Cushing, ME 04563

For Mom and Dad

Chapter 1

Maggie Michaels Wood was preparing for another summer at Chautauqua Institution, New York where her Mother, Ann Michaels, owned a house. Chautauqua Institution stands in the southwestern corner of New York about seventy miles south of Buffalo, New York.

In 1874 two ministers from Ohio visited Chautauqua Lake and set up their ramshackle tents. No indoor bathroom facilities. Electricity hadn't been discovered yet, though Thomas Edison would later marry a Chautauquan. The tents were later raised on platforms made of hemlock. And still later they became cottages with mansard roofs, porticoes, balconies, porches, bay windows and gingerbread trim. In nearby cities of Buffalo and Pittsburgh sixty percent of the people were foreign-born. H. J. Heinz created his company in Pittsburgh. He later purchased a home at Chautauqua Institution. During the summers a great 'white fleet' of steamboats clustered on Lake Chautauqua carrying a new tourist class seeking the next 'watering hole.' Readers of 1874 discovered *The Mysterious Island* by Jules Vernes and Thomas Hardy's *Far from the Madding Crowd*.

Maggie grew up in her parents' home hearing the history

of Chautauqua. Most children knew Chautauqua's history by the time they were six walking to Boys' or Girls' Club for a day of fun.

Maggie's Mother had visited the 'grounds' (as it was affectionately called) with an aunt when she was a little girl. After her aunt died Maggie's Mother continued to visit Chautauqua, staying in rented rooms while raising two daughters. When she was 45, Ann Michaels and Henry Michaels, Maggie's father, purchased a home. He presented it to her Mother on their 25th wedding anniversary. Henry could clean bats out of the attic. He could wire lamps and build shower stalls with poured concrete floors. He could paint and nail any part of the house. One spring day while painting the exterior the ladder collapsed sending Henry violently to the ground. He was buried in the Chautauqua Cemetery the next week.

This was Maggie's sixtieth year on earth and her fifty-fifth at Chautauqua Institution. Maggie's husband David did not like Chautauqua. He never could explain why. He resented both being asked about his reasons and reminded of the few times he had visited. It finally became a topic not to mention. Maggie knew David could suck the breath out of anything. She didn't need David to enjoy Chautauqua.

She could take her place in the front row of the Amphitheater or Bratton Hall Theater, or attend church services and never feel awkward without her husband. But that was part of the charm of Chautauqua. Women could and had lived at Chautauqua for generations without their men. Women bonded at lectures, plays, and symphonies going on every day and night for nine weeks. And if Maggie and all the women Chautauquans didn't feel like talking while sitting

Chautauqua After Hours

on a hard-back bench in the large open-air Amphitheater they knit. And they knit and knit through July and August. Chautauqua had some of the best knitters in the country, though Maggie was not one of them. Her small talent and pleasure lay in oil painting. She hoped to improve her art this season with more classes at the art studio.

Maggie drove through the Main Gate and stopped to get her ticket from the attendant. When a car pulled up at the gate the attendant took it seriously. One could not enter Chautauqua without a gate ticket and a parking pass for the car. Another brick building stood parallel to the road. It housed customer service, the computer station, will call, gate tickets, and rest rooms. Gate tickets for every event were sold here. The whole of Chautauqua's history greeted a visitor as they entered the gate area. There one paid for the privilege to walk on the grounds.

Maggie picked up her parking pass and gate ticket at the window. She drove through the gate. She heard the Miller Bell Tower playing *The Battle Hymn of the Republic*. The Bell Tower, situated down by the lake, was built in 1911 of Italian Campanile. It stood 75 feet tall with an open belfry at the top. A lighted metal clock adorned each side. It rang on the hour, half, quarter, and three-quarter hour. It always tugged at her heart when she heard it...gong...gong...gong. The sound echoed throughout the 365 acres of Chautauqua. Whenever Maggie heard the Bell Tower no matter where she was on the grounds it told her she was away from that 'other world' out there. She was here now. Gong. Gong. Gong. Bell Tower serenade. She could rely on it. The unique history of Chautauqua rang from the belfry into the sky.

Mary Keating

As Maggie drove down Massey Avenue toward James Avenue she wondered if she would stay longer than a month. She hoped David would visit. He could try to change a little and visit for two weeks, couldn't he?

Maggie would stay with her Mother. She enjoyed her Mother at this age. She was turning eighty in two weeks. And Maggie didn't want to waste a minute with any small disagreements. When Maggie was younger they could get into it whenever they both forgot the blood that flowed between them.

Now her Mother was easygoing and seemed to help Maggie with her life situations more than when she was a teen-ager. Maggie loved being in her Mother's home. It always felt like a refuge. She was glad to drive up to the modest Chautauqua house tucked between two larger Victorian homes. Maggie could see her Mother hanging clothes on the clothes hanger behind the house. Maggie walked around the small garden her father had planted.

Hey, Mom.

Honey, you made it.

Chapter 2

A charter bus arrived late at night at the Main Gate. Its engine purred. The attendant waved them through. A round of clapping could be heard inside. On the side of the bus were large posters with *South Pacific* titles. The bus made a turn to the left and stopped at a brown building called Bellinger Hall. The performers disembarked from the bus.

All of them were tired; all of them were persons of color.

Evita, young and stylish, would play Nellie Forbush in the concert. She looked around at her surroundings. She noticed the parking lot nearby.

Hey, Paul look at all them cars. Do you think they'll come see us?

Maybe. Let's get inside and see our digs.

Paul Rains opened the door for Evita. Paul knew Evita wanted to get to know him better but he was older and not interested in an affair during this *South Pacific* concert. Paul was too deep in a divorce from his wife in Mississippi to give out flirtatious signals to Evita.

The cast followed Evita and Paul into Bellinger Hall. The last actress to stroll in was a heavyset woman who would play Bloody Mary.

Inside Bellinger were simple dorm rooms and a large dining area.

Jeremy Stokes, who would play Lieutenant Cable, climbed to the top bunk in the room he would share with Paul. Jeremy lit a cigarette. He blew smoke.

Well whaddya' think, Paul?

Give it a chance, kid. It might be quiet back here behind these gates.

No way, bro, they all white folks.

Jeremy stubbed his cigarette in the ashtray. He laid his head on the pillow. It was quiet now in Bellinger Hall. The singers, all total strangers to Chautauqua Institution, drifted into their own fragments of dreams and nightmares.

Chapter 3

Across 'the grounds' on James Street a party was going on at Ann Michaels' home. The lights shone from the porch and inside. Music blared from the antique phonograph and someone was belting out tunes on the piano.

Maggie circled through the rooms and talked to all the opera singers who had just finished *H.M.S. Pinafore*. *Pinafore* was one of her Mother's favorite productions. Maggie knew that her Mother knew there were strict rules about noise after 11 p.m. Chautauqua was filled with tradition, rules and rituals that generation after generation abided by. Ann Michaels had another way of looking at her parties.

Why couldn't she give back to the very singers who gave the Chautauqua patrons such pleasure at the opera? This was her way. It was now 1 a.m. A siren sounded outside the house. Officer Biggs in his blue shirt and pants stepped from the car. He walked up the four steps of 33 James and knocked on the door.

Ann opened the door.

Hello, Officer Biggs. Won't you come in?

No thank you, ma'am. You know we don't allow parties at this hour. It's the rule.

Uh-huh. Ann Michaels was more bemused than annoyed.

I know you heard this before but this is my way of giving back. You see?

Well, sure but I have to do my job.

And a good job you do, Officer Biggs. Are you sure you won't come in and have some punch?

Oh, no I'll say good night. Please end the party. My boss hates this kind of thing. You know.

Of course, now best get back to your car. Good night.

The singers in the background sang "*Good Night Irene, Good night, Irene, I'll get you in my dreams.*"

Mrs. Michaels shut the door.

The party continued. Maggie watched her childhood friend, Weezie, spin around the room with trays of hors d'oeuvres.

I'm so glad you're here for a month, Maggie, Weezie said.

Gosh, these are so good, Weezie.

Maybe I should cater. Your mom is my best customer. Say is David coming sometime?

Another business trip. You know same old thing. His loss.

Maggie sipped her drink. One of the cast came over to Maggie and asked her to dance. She rose and stepped into his arms. Each time they spun around she could feel her head getting woozy.

I must say good night, Gil, thank you.

Mother you were great again. I'm going up now.

Of course, dear. You need your beauty rest.

Not at this age.

All the more at your age.

Maggie climbed the steps and opened the door to her bed-

Chautauqua After Hours

room. With the party still going on she knew there was no way she was going to sleep. She stepped into the bedroom where her Mother slept and looked out at the park through the windows. She loved the park. The silhouettes of the trees hovered in the darkness of Chautauqua. She stepped to the porch and sat in a wicker chair. The night was breezy. She liked how it bathed her skin. It was July in her Mother's home at Chautauqua and nothing could soothe her more.

    The Bell Tower chimed 2 a.m. Maggie couldn't stay all night on the porch. She went back into her bedroom and fell asleep.

Chapter 4

The next morning the President of Chautauqua held a meeting in his office overlooking Bestor Plaza. The police were in attendance.

Now men, our new visitors arrived last night. As you all know they are people of diversity including a few Asians. This is some big foundation's work to send this group here to perform *South Pacific*. They put up the money. But I am telling you this—we are not going to let any Chautauquan try to make a political issue out of it. You hear me. But just in case I'm adding a few more patrolmen. Jimmy Biggs you report to me.

Yes, sir, Mr. President.

Across from the President's office one could see Bestor Plaza, the heart of the grounds. The Plaza had a fountain with a four-sided sculpture representing art, music, knowledge, and religion in bas-relief panels on each side. Sculptures of fish and doves sat at each end spouting water into the fountain. The ritual of throwing pennies into the blue water of the Bestor Plaza Fountain had kept children delighted for over 100 years.

Jeremy hung over the side of the fountain. Paul stood near

Chautauqua After Hours

him.

Look at 'em. Shiny money.

Lucky pennies.

They just sunk on down with all them wishes. Jeremy reached into the water to grab a penny.

Hey.

Paul tried to grab him back.

Officer Biggs appeared. He grabbed harder than Paul and threw Jeremy's body to the ground.

You stay out of that fountain, what's your name?

Jeremy Stokes.

He's with the singers, sir. We're here for *South Pacific*.

I know what you're here for. Don't give him the right to go in the fountain.

Yes, sir. Paul tossed a penny in the fountain.

Now that's more like it. They stay there once you make a wish. It's a kid's magnet.

Got it.

Now you best head back to Bellinger.

Jeremy started to walk away but stopped by a tree.

Paul walked away toward the Chautauqua Bookstore under the Post Office. Officer Biggs walked down the redbrick walk toward the Backstage Cafe for a cup of coffee.

Jeremy waited until Biggs was out of sight. He walked back to the fountain and sat down in one of the couches nearby. He watched an older woman with a toddler. He hummed a few lines of *Younger Than Springtime*. Hmmm. Hmmm.

The woman lifted the child to the fountain and let the little boy throw a penny in the water.

Make a wish sweetheart.

The little boy nodded his head.

Jeremy, fascinated by the ritual, called out. Is that your grandson, ma'am?

The older woman lifted the toddler down. She put the child in the stroller. She rolled the stroller to the other side of the fountain.

Jeremy rose from the couch. He walked toward the woman.

Excuse me, ma'am....what do these figures mean here on the statue?

How rude, if you don't move along I will call the police.

The police? I was just trying to learn about this fountain.

There's a bookstore right over there. It will teach you all you want to know. Now please leave me alone. Shouldn't you be at work somewhere?

Yeah, I's doing the garbage trucks ma'am and singing all the time while I's picking up white trash.

Jeremy walked away.

The woman picked up her cell phone. She called Officer Biggs.

Yes, he was just here bothering me. I don't know who he is but he said he worked on the garbage trucks. See to it he is reprimanded. And remember I'm not a whistleblower.

Got it ma'am. I'll be right over.

Jeremy walked toward the bookstore. Just as he was about to enter Officer Biggs called out to him.

Hey you, Jeremy.

Jeremy stopped cold.

Come with me.

What charge? I'm here with *South Pacific*...with the con-

cert here.
 You harassed a fifth-generation grandmother.
 I was talking. What you mean, harassed?
 Stop the lip. Get in the car.
 Officer Biggs shoved Jeremy in the back seat. He drove fifty feet to the Police Station behind the Colonnade Building.

Chapter 5

P aul stood near the biography section. He picked out a book on Nelson Mandela. Chautauquans noticed him.

Maggie perused the theater section. She adored musicals so she was quite excited that this troupe had arrived at Chautauqua. It had been written about in *The Daily*, Chautauqua's newspaper during the summer season. The article had explained that a foundation in New York had put up the money to try something very new and exciting. They were sending people of diversity to Chautauqua to sing songs from *South Pacific*. It had never been done before anywhere else in the country. Maggie glowed with pride that Chautauqua was finally seeing into the Zeitgeist out there. There had been a few preachers of color over 145 years but not nearly enough. She heard there was one property owner now after 145 years. The only other persons of color were young actors and dancers and now two young writers-in-residence.

Maggie picked out an Andrew Lloyd Webber memoir. She rounded the shelving and bumped into a tall handsome man. There was a pause. Paul was the first to speak.

I'm sorry. Excuse me.

Chautauqua After Hours

Oh, I wasn't paying attention. I get lost in books. Don't you?

Books will do that.

It got quiet. Maggie couldn't think of what to say. She smiled.

After you.

Oh, I'm going to the back of the store, she explained.

She had changed her mind and decided not to stand at the cash register behind or in front of this man. It would be more awkward than it already was. Then he spoke again.

I'm Paul Rains.

As in Claude Rains?

Paul chuckled. Yes.

I'm Maggie Michaels Wood. I'm so glad you've come to Chautauqua.

Maggie looked at the book Paul was buying. She really had to buy paints for her class and this conversation wasn't going anywhere.

I'll see you, nice to meet you.

Maggie dashed off to the back of the bookstore. She purchased a few oil paints and brushes. She tried not to hear her heart pounding.

Chapter 6

Maggie followed the red-brick walk toward the back of the Amphitheater. The Amphitheater was the famous open-sided, performance center on the grounds. Franklin D. Roosevelt, Amelia Earhart, Robert Kennedy, John Denver, Joan Baez and hundreds of other famous people had spoken or performed from its wide, hallowed, wooden stage.

Weezie now owned the Backstage Cafe located across from the Amphitheater. Maggie loved Weezie. She was a good and loyal friend from childhood. They had gone to Girls' Club together where they sang: "*Onward Girls' Club, Onward Boys' Club full of life and pep cheerful ever solemn never that's our Girls' Club rep rah rah rah*"— each morning. The wooden building down by the lake was the center for activities throughout the day.

Weezie never married but she had serious relationships she shared with Maggie. Maggie kept Weezie informed of her ups and downs with David.

Maggie walked in. Weezie came from behind the sink and handed Maggie a brownie.

I just baked them.

You are going to get me fat.

Chautauqua After Hours

What did they say to the women on the *Titanic*? They should have eaten dessert first.
Morbid.
Are you still giving your Mom a birthday party?
Sure am. In a week.
Let me help.
Sure. Want to make the cake? She loves lemon cake.
Done. Where will you have the party?
At the St. Elmo. It isn't a surprise, that would be impossible with Mom.
Say, did you see any of the singers here for *South Pacific*?
I did see one in the bookstore.
I'm serving them coffee and donuts and brownies after hours.
Oh, I love those late rehearsals in the Amp.
Come over then.
Maybe.

Chapter 7

Paul sat on his beach towel near the Bell Tower eating a peach. A young life guard sat in his chair looking all around at the young women on the beach. One young woman swam out toward the raft.

She paddled around and around in a circle then suddenly she began to scream.

Help. Help. I can't move.

Paul threw his peach away and jumped in the water. He swam out toward the young woman. He dove down into the green seaweed. It was dark. He could barely see the woman's legs tangled by the seaweed. A fish swam by. The woman continued to scream.

Paul grabbed a handful of seaweed and unknotted it from her legs. Then he pulled at the seaweed to loosen it from the bottom of the lake. His strong hands reached for the woman under her arms. He guided her into shore.

The lifeguard stood in the shallow water. He took the woman from Paul.

Where were you? God, who is this?

Have no idea. But Tiffany he did come rescue you.

That's your job, Petey.

Chautauqua After Hours

The young woman walked away toward the police car parked near the Bell Tower.

Officer, would you do something? He came after me.

What d'ya mean?

Arrest him or I'll have my father call the President.

Officer Roland, a short, beefy, man walked to Paul. He pointed at him. Paul stood dead still.

This young woman, Tiffany Hegland, says there was some funny business under water.

Paul stared straight ahead.

Well, what have you to say for yourself?

Hey, Officer, he just got her free of the seaweed, chimed Petey.

Thanks, Petey, I'll tell you when I need your opinion.

Paul patted his bare chest. He took a deep breath.

Come with me fellow, I'll take you up to police headquarters till we get this straightened out.

Paul walked with Officer Roland. Roland escorted him to the back seat.

Officer Roland drove off.

Chapter 8

Jeremy sat in a holding area. Roland walked in with Paul. He showed him into the same room where Jeremy was being held.

Paul and Jeremy looked at each other.

Roland and Officer Biggs walked into another office and shut the door.

Biggs picked up a pencil and started tapping it on the desk.

God this isn't good. The President is going to have our balls.

Hegland's daughter, Tiffany what was I supposed to do? A member of the board, Christ sake. She says he was leering or something underwater.

Oh, that's smart. You can't see shit underwater in that goddamn seaweed!

What you got?

Some grandmother at the fountain one of our venerable older generations tells me he's harassing her.

Jesus, what do we do?

We're talking singers in *South Pacific*. The phone rang.

Yes, Mr. Hegland, yes, she was quite upset. Hysterical? Well maybe. He's a singer here to perform. No charges? Yes,

Chautauqua After Hours

I will tell him. Whatever you say, Mr. Hegland.
 Roland hung up.
 No charges.
 I got no proof on this kid Jeremy but I had a run-in with him this morning. Let's get them out of here. The sooner the show is over the better.
 Roland and Biggs walked over to the prisoners. They let them out of the room.
 I don't know if you were helping or what but next time let the lifeguard do his job, said Officer Roland.
 I told you to stay away from that fountain this morning. One more time and I arrest you show or no show, threatened Biggs.
 Paul and Jeremy left the headquarters and walked up to the red-brick walk toward Bellinger Hall.
 As they passed by Victorian homes, Bratton Theater and Norton Hall, Jeremy noticed a large wooden sign on a porch graced with vases of gladioli.
 CHAUTAUQUA: THE MOST AMERICAN PLACE IN THE COUNTRY!
 Would you look at that bullshit? Come on, what's the matter with these people? Where are we? Huh? What do ya think Paul?
 I think I met my woman.
 What? Man, you're a goner.

Chapter 9

Maggie left Weezie's cafe and looked forward to a morning chat with her Mother. When she arrived at the house she could see there was company. Not exactly company but her younger sister, Lauren. Hank, Lauren's seventeen-year-old son, with carrot-top hair, was unpacking the bags from Lauren's car.

Maggie kissed her sister and nephew.

Great you're here.

Come in, sweetheart, Hank, Maggie. Let's all sit down for a cup of coffee.

Maggie followed her Mother into the house and put her books on the hallway table.

More books, Maggie? Lauren asked.

You bet.

They all walked into the kitchen. Ann poured fresh coffee she had brewed earlier.

Let me look at you, Hank. You've grown like a weed.

I have Grandma.

Mom, I'm going down to the docks. Gotta see the SCOT.

Okay, honey. Just make sure the car is locked.

You don't need to worry about your car, dear. You're at

Chautauqua After Hours

Chautauqua!
 Oh, right, forgot. Hank left the kitchen.
 So what's new?   Lauren asked.
 Oh we had the police here again, of course, one of Mom's parties.
 Lauren laughed.
 Listen girls, I want you both to join me this afternoon for the strawberry shortcake festival at the Women's Club.
 I'm in.
 I really can't Mom, I have to unpack and I'm supposed to help Hank at the boat.
 Ann looked disappointed.
 Maggie be sure to wear a pretty dress.
 Maggie gave her Mom that look she'd given her her whole life. But then she remembered her Mother was nearly eighty so she let it go.
 When she painted Maggie would wear her smock and dungarees.

Chapter 10

Maggie set up her easel and sat on her little stool and began to paint the Bell Tower. She loved plein-air. Quick with the oils. Penetrating the moment.

Maggie could not see Paul playing Frisbee on the other side of the Bell Tower. The way the College Club was situated to the right of the Bell Tower, it blocked the view of the small beach and swimming area.

Many singers from *South Pacific* were soaking up the sun. Paul caught the Frisbee from a crew member. He tossed it back. The crew member threw it hard. It skimmed past Paul toward the other side of the College Club. It landed near Maggie.

You get it, Keith, Paul directed.

No way, bro' you see all those cop cars over there?

Paul gave him a look. He walked toward the other side of the College Club.

Maggie looked up to see Paul approaching her easel. He was coming toward her private space now.

How he could do this without her running bothered Maggie. Paul quietly came up to her and bent over. He grabbed the Frisbee and looked at Maggie. He glanced at her painting. Respectful. He smiled and left.

Maggie stood up and walked around in a circle. She looked at the painting. She looked at the Bell Tower. Then she heard it. Gong. Gong. Twice. It was 2 o'clock. This man, Paul, had just come over to her and not said a word. How considerate. Most people stood and gawked and asked a lot of annoying questions when they saw her painting. Most of the time they were not painters and seemed to want a free lesson about something they would never try. He had gone. The Bell Tower was now playing *Beautiful Dreamer* and Maggie was gathering her paints and brushes and running to the Women's Club.

Chapter 11

Maggie walked through the garden of the Women's Club. She saw her Mother talking with friends. As Maggie approached the table to check-in she noticed a copy of *The Daily*. In a small side at the bottom: *Two Singers in South Pacific Held by Police*. Maggie read on.

Two leading singers in South Pacific, Paul Rains and Jeremy Stokes, were held by police and later released with no charge. Each incident involved a Chautauquan and the singer.

Both singers will perform at the Amphitheater August 1-5 in the South Pacific concert. Extra police have been assigned during the time the singers are on the grounds.

Ann walked up to Maggie.

I know I know I didn't have time to change, Mom. Did you see this in *The Daily*?

I did. Actors or singers I guess, have no business fraternizing with Chautauquans. They know better. My goodness. They are artists. Jumping into the water to get seaweed off? Goodness!

What are you talking about?

Well they didn't print it but I heard from Gretchen one of them went in the water to get seaweed off the Hegland girl,

Chautauqua After Hours

what's her name Samantha, Tiffany?
   Tiffany. Really?
   Come on let's get our shortcake and lemonade. I see Gretchen.
   Maggie followed her Mother over to a table and sat down. She forked into her strawberry shortcake and smiled.
   Gretchen, wearing a pretty dress with sandals on her feet, sat down next to Maggie and across from Ann.
   Been painting, Maggie?
   The Bell Tower.
   Good for you. I hear there's a party happening soon.
   Oh, Maggie won't let me go quietly into my 80's.
   Gretchen laughed. What can I bring?
   Yourself. The St. Elmo has it all covered for food.
   Maggie took another bite of the strawberry shortcake. She smiled again.
   Maggie, it's always delicious, chimed her Mother.

Chapter 12

Shower time. Hank and Lauren playfully passed each other in the upstairs hall dressed in their bathrobes. Lauren had curlers in her long hair. She won the rush to the bathroom.

Hank, take your shower downstairs.

Right, am I supposed to wear a tie?

Ask your aunt.

Hank shouted toward Maggie's bedroom. Do I need to wear a tie, Maggie?

No, a shirt and long pants are fine.

Maggie placed three dresses on her bed. She held each one up to her body. She looked in the mirror on the back of the door. She decided on the blue dress.

Mom, I'll be right in to help you.

Okay, dear.

Lauren stepped out of the bathroom in a towel. She left her bathrobe in the bathroom, then walked into her bedroom and quickly threw on her dress. She put a little blush and lipstick on, and earrings.

Mom, are you ready? Hank, are you downstairs? Maggie, are you bringing Mom? Lauren asked from the hallway.

Chautauqua After Hours

Hank called upstairs. I'm down here and ready.

Okay, I'll join you. Mom, it's going to be a great party. Maggie called down the hall.

I'll be right along with Mom.

Maggie stood behind her Mother and brushed her hair. Ann drank a glass of wine.

Mom, isn't it early?

Not for wine, Maggie. Never for wine.

Are you excited about the party?

I am dear, I do love a party, you know that.

Maggie tried to imagine the party. She thought about the fact her husband David was not coming. She shrugged off that thought. Then she had another thought while wistfully brushing her Mother's hair.

Will he be rehearsing at the Amphitheater after hours?

Chapter 13

Maggie and Ann walked through the park and headed for the St. Elmo. The St. Elmo sat proud as a peacock on Bestor Plaza. Though it used to be a Victorian hotel it was now condos with shops underneath. A small restaurant in the St. Elmo was set up for the party.

Hank looked out the side French doors to watch for the guest of honor, his Grandma. Inside, the room was festive with flowers and balloons. A piano player sat in the corner playing *What I Did For Love*. A large lemon cake sat in the middle of the table with the words *Happy Birthday Mom*, written across the middle. Eighty colorful candles sat on top.

Maggie walked toward the steps leading up to the restaurant. Ann held onto her arm lightly. She hesitated.

Whew, I'm a little woozy, must be the wine.

Just four steps up, Mom. Take one at a time.

Maggie could hear the music inside. The piano player sounded talented. She was glad.

Yes, dear.

Her mother stumbled going up.

Can't do it, Maggie. Get some help.

I'll guide your feet.

Chautauqua After Hours

Maggie bent down to her Mother's feet. She helped her step up. Ann held onto Maggie. The party just twenty feet away. There was a heavy slump and down. Maggie screamed.

Mom, Mom, what?

She bent to her Mother lying unconscious on the porch. Hank rushed outside.

Maggie, what's wrong with Grandma?

Call an ambulance, Hank. Hank took out his cell and called 911. Lauren rushed out to the porch.

Oh, my God, Mom. She knelt down to her Mother.

What is it, Maggie?

Hank began CPR. He handed his cell to Lauren.

Here, call them again.

Hello, we need to get an ambulance here at the St. Elmo right away, 80 years old, yes, and she's my Mother.

Maggie stood up and looked around and around.

Where are they? Where are they? It's just up the road they're just up at the gate.

Friends began to gather at the French doors.

Lauren got up and walked inside the restaurant.

Maggie bent down again.

Mom, hold on, please hold on. Is she breathing, Hank?

Maggie could hardly stand up when the ambulance arrived. Her legs had gone weak on her.

The EMTs did their work and then they lifted Mrs. Ann Michaels into the ambulance to take her away to the hospital in the next town, Westfield. Hank helped Maggie climb in alongside her Mother.

The sirens sounded as the ambulance pulled away leaving

Mary Keating

Lauren and Hank and the guests standing in the night air. Questions floated around the room: what went wrong? Would Ann live?

Chapter 14

Four days later Maggie stepped from the funeral home's limousine to the porch of 33 James. Her Mother was dead. She was buried. Maggie was numb all over. Lauren and Hank and friends gathered inside the house where a large spread of food lay on the dining room table.

When Maggie walked in Hank took her hand and placed it near his heart. Maggie hugged her nephew. She poured herself a drink. Everyone whispered. No one played the piano. Lauren was drinking. Her voice was the loudest in the room.

Maggie excused herself and went upstairs. She laid down on her Mother's bed. Her breathing stretched into the room and out beyond the second floor porch to the grass of the park; to the grass of Bestor Plaza; to the lapping water at the Bell Tower; and to the garden at the Women's Club and that lovely day of strawberry shortcake.

She heard her shoes drop to the floor. She wondered if her father knew what was happening to him when he died? Her father made it all possible that Chautauqua lived for all of them. The worker bee who often could not join the family at Chautauqua because he had to work extra to make the money to pay the mortgage on the house at Chautauqua.

Mary Keating

Maggie cried into her pillow.

Chapter 15

The next morning Lauren was up bright and early packed and ready to leave. She walked around the dining room table looking at all the leftover food. Hank ran in and out packing the car. Lauren packed a few sandwiches for the two of them.

Make sure the trunk is closed, honey.

I will, Mom.

Lauren walked up the stairs. She looked in Maggie's bedroom. Empty. She opened the door to her Mother's room and found Maggie.

Maggie's grief-stricken face hardly responded to the woman entering the room. Lauren held a pair of tennis shoes in her hand.

I'm going Maggie. I can't take being here now.

Can't take it?

I'm too down, you know I don't like to be down, and Hank's remedial classes...I really can't stay in Mom's house right now.

Lauren's eyes welled up. Maggie looked nowhere.

You let me know what you want to do with the house.

What can you mean?

My god, Maggie, Mom's gone.
He couldn't even come to the funeral.
Yeah, what's with that? I thought David liked Mom. I may be back in a couple of weeks. Not sure.
Maggie stared right through Lauren.
Okay, then I'll see you...Mom had a good life.
Maggie rose from the bed.
A good life?
Yeee—ah.
I don't need your shallow philosophy now, Lauren.
Oh, sure you have it all figured out right. Your beliefs are smarter, always think you're smarter.
I can't be with you now.
Good, 'cuz I'm leaving.
Lauren turned and rushed out the door.
Maggie stepped onto the second-floor porch and watched her go. Maggie turned back to the room. She put on her Mother's bathrobe and sat in a chair. She liked the smell of her Mother's bathrobe, the comfort of it. She ran her fingers down the arms and felt the soft chenille under her fingertips. She pulled the tie tighter and slumped low in the chair.

After a few hours she got up and walked downstairs. She went to the kitchen and boiled water for tea. Next she opened the cupboard for the peanut butter and jelly.

Maggie toasted the whole-wheat bread then spread the peanut butter and strawberry jelly on top. The water boiled.

Maggie opened the china cabinet and took out one of her Mother's china tea cups. She fixed her tea with milk and sat down. In front of her eyes was a vase of gladioli. Pink. They were haggard and needed to be thrown away. Maggie stood

Chautauqua After Hours

up and pitched the glads in the trashcan outside. Now she was standing right at the clothes contraption her Mother found in a yard sale. It was the ugliest old thing. Some kind of rusted metal that swung around and around with long hanger-like arms for the clothes. But she felt keenly how much her Mother loved it. Then. Now Maggie ached for her Mother and loved the old thing too.

She would do a load of wash in the washer and hang clothes out to dry. Maggie wondered how this idea had come to her in her numbed state but she was glad for the activity.

She looked up and saw Gretchen coming toward her from Forest Avenue.

Gretchen gave Maggie a hug.
I'm so sorry, Maggie.
I don't know what to do.
I know, I know.
What do we do, you've lost your Mother too.
We remember. Remember everything.

Gretchen walked through the alley between houses to Forest.

Maggie walked inside to begin the wash. She would not make it to the Amphitheater this morning. Suddenly she didn't care who was speaking.

Chapter 16

Every morning there was a lecture in the Amphitheater. Every night there was an event. It could be a pop concert, classical music, a dance company, or a famous entertainer. Someone would introduce the lecturer in the morning, usually the President of Chautauqua. At night the audiences buzzed in conversation until the performance started. The audiences clapped for every performance. Most everyone got a standing ovation.

Afterwards, around 11 p.m., the stage crew shut down the lighting and sound system. But when a special performance needed to rehearse after hours, the crew left the lights dim and the sound system low.

The singers stood on the stage. A conductor tapped his baton, the small orchestra played *Some Enchanted Evening* softly.

Paul walked to the front of the stage. He began to sing the song quietly.

The conductor swung his baton then he suddenly signaled to stop. Paul stopped singing.

Let's go back three bars. Strings, watch tempo.

They played the romantic song again. Paul sang the words

again. The conductor let the orchestra continue. Orchestra and Paul were in sync. Paul finished the song.

Good, good, we'll break and come back late tomorrow. We're almost there. Not to worry. Only three more days to rehearse.

Chapter 17

At night Maggie's wash still blew in the wind. The moon spread its luster through the trees. Silhouettes shifted to and fro.

Maggie tossed in a dream:

She sees her Mother, young and lovely, in a summer dress and heels, with her brown hair blowing in the wind. She looks down at Maggie from the second-floor porch. Maggie stands near the purple flowers and looks up at her Mother. Maggie is seven.

Follow the red-brick walk, sweetheart. You'll see it.

Red, Mommy, I thought it was yellow.

This one's red. You'll see. Stay on the red-brick walk to the post office.

Okay Mommy.

Maggie turns and skips away down James to the red-brick walk. She finds it. End of dream.

Maggie woke up and walked to the bathroom to take a shower. She pulled on a pretty summer dress and flats and walked down the hallway. She stood for a moment at the top of the stairs. She hesitated. Then she walked down to the front door.

Chautauqua After Hours

Maggie stood outside. She turned and looked at the house. The sun began to come around the corner. A large leafy maple stood to the left of the garden of flowers and tomatoes. Maggie headed down James to the red-brick walk. She stopped and looked at her feet.

I'm here.

Now her dream guided her. She took a left toward Bestor Plaza and the Post Office. Other Chautauquans walked toward the Amphitheater for the morning lecture.

Young teen-age boys called out "Get your *Chautauquan Daily*, get your *Chautauquan Daily*".

Maggie stopped and bought one. She noticed the young boy had a tattoo.

Maggie climbed the steep steps to the Post Office. She walked to the window to pick up her Mother's mail.

Helen, the postmaster who was about to retire, greeted Maggie at the window.

We're so sorry, so sorry, Maggie.

Thank you, Helen.

Your Mom is going to be missed for a long time.

Maggie couldn't say more.

I'll just get your Mom's mail.

Helen brought a large pile of magazines and newspapers back. Maggie took them in a bag. She walked back along the red-brick walk. She wouldn't stop to hear the lecture.

Chapter 18

Maggie turned into the Backstage Cafe. She sat at a small ice-cream table. Weezie brought her a small salad and iced coffee.

Oh, thanks Weezie. I could use some nourishment. I can't seem to cook anything.

It's okay, Maggie, you know I love to make simple things. I see you got the mail.

Yeah, lots of it. I probably will throw it all away. Mom loved her magazines.

It's just too hard to believe.

Maggie bit into her salad.

Are you going to come tonight?

What?

Remember I stay open for the singers and they come round for coffee and dessert. Singers...the people your Mom loved.

I don't know...I'm not feeling real social.

I know.

Chapter 19

Maggie stepped up to the front porch. She opened the front door. The phone rang.

Hello, Lauren, well that's how it is.

David, no show not yet. Is Hank coming back with you? I see. Good-bye.

Maggie sat down on the living room rug and emptied the bag of mail. She opened an eighteen-month calendar of cats. She tossed it across the room. She got up and walked to the kitchen. Now she would clean. She put on gloves and filled a bucket with Pine Sol and hot water. She scrubbed the kitchen floor. Then she scrubbed the bathroom clean. When she finished she climbed the stairs to make her Mother's bed up with clean sheets. Exhausted she laid down and fell asleep.

When she awoke it was 11:15 p.m. Wide awake now, Maggie remembered Weezie telling her about the singers. She washed her face and dressed. She walked out the door.

When Maggie arrived at the Backstage Cafe it was full of the cast from *South Pacific*. She found Weezie.

Oh, this is so good, I'm so glad you came.

Maggie sat down in the corner. Jeremy walked over to her table.

Is this seat taken?
No, it's yours.
Jeremy dragged the chair over to another table.
Weezie brought Maggie a cup of coffee.
Did you see that article in *The Daily*? What a crime.
I did. Something's not right here, Weezie.
Paul walked in. Maggie settled down in the back corner. She saw him move along the counter. He picked up coffee, brownies and a bottle of water. He drank the water as if he were parched from heat.
Maggie watched Weezie talking to Paul. Then they turned and began to come over to the corner. *No. They were coming her way.* Maggie sat still. She had *The Daily* on her table.
Let me introduce you.
Oh we met in the bookstore.
Briefly.
Hello again. Paul noticed *The Daily*.
I guess the news has gotten around.
Oh, no I mean I have no idea. I don't really know what they're talking about.
I was helping a young woman out of the seaweed.
Seaweed?
Yes.
Of course, it's thick and nasty now.
The seaweed?
Yes.
I really must be going. Good night.
Paul looked at Weezie.
She's going through a hard time now, her Mother just died two weeks ago.

Chautauqua After Hours

Then help me out, Weezie, where can I find a florist?
Westfield. I have their number.
I'll call tomorrow. Where does Maggie live?
33 James Avenue.

Chapter 20

Maggie pinned her hair up. She turned an Aretha Franklin classic up loud on the phonograph. She opened the windows. As she looked at the white walls she took her brush of yellow paint and made a big swoosh over the wall. It made her feel better. Then she climbed up the ladder.

Maggie, Maggie, I'm here.

Lauren climbed the stairs with tennis shoes in her hand. Lauren stood in the bedroom.

Come on Maggie, put that down and come play tennis with me.

What?

Tennis.

Can't you see I'm painting? I'm painting the whole room yellow.

I see. Not my color but whatever. You never play tennis with me anymore.

We haven't played since College Club days, Lauren.

Okay, then I'm going down to the docks. Hank is here with me. He's so excited to be racing in the regatta.

How long are you staying?

Maggie climbed down the ladder. She stumbled on the

Chautauqua After Hours

last step. She cut her ankle.
 That's what you get for asking me such a rude question. Have you forgotten this is my house too?
 Look what you made me do. Rude? It's an ordinary question especially with you always in and out, Maggie said.
 I didn't make you do anything.
 Could you go get me a band-aid? Please.
 Yeah, where?
 In Mom's room. On the bureau. A little dish.
 Maggie sucked the blood off her finger. She knew the dangers of walking into her Mother's room now, the emptiness and darkness there without her Mother's life pulsating. But she doubted if Lauren would feel anything like that.
 Lauren returned with a band-aid.
 Thanks. Maggie pulled it apart and placed it on her ankle.
 Is David coming?
 He is. Around dinner.
 Oh, boy.
 The doorbell rang.
 Maggie jumped up with brush in hand.
 I'll get it.
 I guess you'll live.
 Maggie rushed downstairs to the screen door.
 A large white box lay on the porch. Maggie opened it. Pink gladioli.
 She read the card.
 Please accept my sympathy in this time of great loss. Paul.
 Maggie smiled. She walked back inside to the kitchen. She cut the ends off and placed the glads in a tall vase with water. She carried them back to the porch and set them on a

small wicker table. Then she lingered for a moment; conscious of being a true Chautauquan with glads on her porch.

A thin bittersweet thread of happiness seemed to hover in the midst of her grief.

Chapter 21

Early evening David stood on the porch with his briefcase in his hand. Maggie sat in her chair drinking wine. He was well-dressed, fit but not too fit, with dishwater blond hair that hung over his green eyes. He bent down to give Maggie a peck on the cheek.

I know I know. I have no excuse. But work, darling. I'm sorry I couldn't be here for the funeral. It couldn't be helped.

I think I deserve to be in a mood.

You do. Whatever you need. But can we call a truce now that I'm here?

Come in, dinner's waiting. Maggie held the door for David as he walked through with his small piece of luggage and briefcase.

Not staying long I see?

A week maybe.

Maggie closed the door.

They proceeded to the dining room table that could seat ten. Lauren rushed to David and gave him a big splashy kiss and hug.

Whoa, hello to you, Lauren.

Sit down, David. Lauren showed him a seat. Lauren sat down next to him. Maggie sat on the opposite side.
Let me freshen up.
He walked around the corner to the small bathroom. He used the toilet then he turned to look in the mirror. He washed his face and hands and returned to the seat next to Lauren. David avoided looking at Maggie. Candles flickered.
Maggie picked at her cold meat loaf.
It's really good, Maggie.
It's takeout, David, from the Lighthouse.
Lauren picked up the wine bottle.
More wine, David?
Sure.
Lauren poured David another glass.
You really know your wines, Lauren.
I try. It's being out West, I get down to Sonoma whenever I can.
I wish you'd been here, for Mom's funeral. Where were you? Maggie blurted out loud.
Maggie. Let it go now, Lauren interjected.
I couldn't darling, the big merger was going on, David explained.
Sure, gone. Gone—all gone. Maggie complied.
What's for dessert, Maggie?
Strawberries and this house is not for sale.
Of course it isn't who said anything about that? For goodness sake, Maggie, just get your mind off business now.
Just making sure.
Forget it. Why don't we all go over to Weezie's? You remember Weezie, don't you David?

Chautauqua After Hours

Of course, sure, it hasn't been that long.

Yes, it has. Besides Weezie is busy with the cast from *South Pacific*, Maggie reminded them.

Great maybe we can meet some of them. Besides she has the best brownies on the grounds. Lauren got up.

South Pacific? Maggie, one of your favorites, right? David asked.

I'm not sure you'll think it cool, David.

Why not?

Well, they're doing it rather avant-grade.

David waited for her to say more. Nothing came.

Yes, avant-grade? He repeated her phrasing.

It's a concert you see, like they did once at Carnegie Hall. And they are all persons of diversity. You see?

David knew what Maggie was doing.

You bitch, really, Maggie.

I'm not. I'm merely explaining what is going on here at Chautauqua.

David rose from the table.

Are you coming to Weezie's?

No both of you go on. My feet hurt from climbing the ladder. I'm going to take a long bath. David, you can sleep in the guest room while the paint dries. I'll be in Mom's room.

David and Lauren looked at each other. They walked out.

Maggie sat with the dripping candles. She waited until she heard the door close. Then she blew the candles out. Darkness.

She walked upstairs and drew a bubble bath. She picked up a sympathy card from the floor and read it.

'Know that your loved one is in a better place.'

Mary Keating

Maggie submerged the card underwater. It ran inky blue.

Chapter 22

In the morning Maggie ate her cereal and blueberries alone in the kitchen. She saw a note left by Lauren.

Over at Weezie's—we let you sleep.

Maggie finished her cereal and walked across the park. There were buses dropping off young children to their homes after their morning activities. Maggie smiled at the children.

When she walked into the Backstage Cafe she could see Lauren and David in the back area hunched over their coffees. She saw David look up and watch her. Maggie joined them. She looked down at the table.

Maggie, have some coffee.

Weezie appeared with a fresh pot and mug for Maggie. She poured Maggie's coffee.

Good morning or is it afternoon, Weezie?

Either time I still make the coffee. It sure brings in the singers huh, Maggie?

Oh, I'm sorry I ran off.

It's okay, he wasn't upset I explained about your Mom.

Lauren, dying of curiosity, asked, who's he?

Come on, who is he?

Weezie answered for Maggie.

Oh, the singers last night from *South Pacific*.

Maggie looked at David, watching his expression. She couldn't read his face, so calm, now, after their first night in the house together. She wondered why he was always so calm? He nodded a tiny bit when he heard Weezie explain. Could it be her harebrained sister calmed him down? That would be just like David, to get mixed up with Lauren somehow in some innocent flirtation. Lauren was always one for flirtations. Flirtations that led to two ruined marriages and one son. Of course Hank was a dear, sweet young man. Lauren did have that joy despite her failed marriages.

Maggie's thoughts came back to the table. She caught half a smile from David. Then she heard Lauren.

About Mom's clothes.

Clothes, what?

There are women who do this kind of thing.

No, I don't want any of them in the house. I can do it myself, what's the rush, Lauren?

I can help. I've made arrangements for a week, David added.

I said I'm not ready!!

Okay, what about the house, Maggie? You know I don't want it even if it is in the will.

Is this what the two of you have been talking about here this morning?

Sort of.

Hey, Lauren, I'll give you a loan 'til we figure this out.

David, please stay out of this. The house is to blood, not husbands or ex-husbands, just Lauren and me. You see?

Maggie looked at David. She knew she was glaring at

Chautauqua After Hours

him, as if that would make up for him missing her Mother's funeral. She thought he probably wanted to hear more about the will, but there was nothing more she felt like saying. It didn't seem so strange to her that she just blurted out the will's stipulations right here and now. The house was hers and Lauren's. And deep down Maggie was glad her Mother had written the will this way. It made it less complicated. So now Lauren could just figure out what she wanted to do if she didn't want the house. Was it a loss of nerve on Lauren's part? Or was her heart so shallow that she couldn't see the continuity she had in Hank as a Chautauquan in future generations? No matter. Maggie loved her Mother for leaving it to just the two of them.

David, you really should come visit me in Seattle, on one of your business trips.

Washington? Why would we come to Washington? Lauren?

I'm going to play tennis, want to play a set with me, David?

No, I'm running.

He turned to Maggie and spoke softly.

I didn't realize the will was just blood.

Maggie looked at him for a long time. If she tried really hard she could get back to the time she fell in love with him in Ithaca, New York. They were both students at Cornell and she had a part-time job in the library. They had had some sweet moments when they were young. But lately it took all of her imagination to remember them. Her honeymoon wasn't what all the romantic movies made it out to be. So long ago. Memories would get her nothing this morning. She

Mary Keating

let them go.
    She heard David's voice.
    Good to see you, Weezie. And then he was gone.

Chapter 23

David crossed the park toward 33 James and spotted Lauren sitting on a bench.
David sat down with her.
You okay?
Yeah, I just can't believe Maggie. Mom sure approved of you, David.
That's because I didn't spout off about all the Presbyterians and Methodists and Baptists.
Lauren laughed.
You're right.
They looked at each other.
Do you think Maggie is losing it?
Well, she was close to her Mom, and this is a first. I have nothing to go by. I was too young to remember when my Mother died.
Would you like my share of the house?
Are you kidding? It would be illegal and too complicated on so many levels. No.
Maggie is going to stay here. It's just a feeling.
You mean after the season?
Yeah, I guess.

No, she'd get bored. She'll be back in Ithaca. Too much going on there to stay here. I know she retired early but she's got volunteer committees she loves.   It's deserted here.
Too damn quiet for me.
Me too.
I've got to run.
Lauren looked at his feet.
Man those are old shoes.
Yeah, gotta get some new ones.
Let's go over to Bemus for a drink sometime while you're here. I can't stay in the house all the time.
Okay.

Chapter 24

Maggie had put her swimsuit on under her summer dress.

She stood at the gazebo on the red-brick walk reading the *South Pacific* poster. She saw the group shot of the singers and could pick out Paul. Then she continued on the red-brick walk to the Hall of Philosophy. A speaker was talking about Hollywood and War. She walked in and noticed Gretchen. Maggie sat next to her. She heard a few words about the unreality of Hollywood in all the famous war scenes. She looked at Gretchen and shook her head 'no'.

Maggie got up quietly and walked out. She continued back down the red-brick walk past the Smith Wilkes building. Inside there was a one-woman show on Susan B. Anthony. Maggie stood at the back and listened for a moment. Even Susan B. Anthony could not hold her attention now. She stepped back on James then down the hill toward the Athenaeum. She watched the garbage men pick up trash from the back of the hotel. The trucks opened and dumped the cans of trash. It quite mesmerized Maggie. Now she walked toward the Women's Club and on toward the lake. She passed the Sports' Club and Palestine Park with the replica of the

Mary Keating

Holy Land, then headed toward the Bell Tower. There she found a bench where she opened a book and began to read.

Chapter 25

Paul laid on his bunkbed smoking a cigarette. There was a knock at the door.

Come in.

Evita, dressed in shorts and a pretty top, stood in the doorway.

Hey.

Hey.

You think we need to rehearse up here for an hour before tonight?

No, we don't, we know it inside and out.

Evita moved toward Paul's cot.

Then let's just hang out together. 'Cuz I got the jitters. What if there's trouble?

There isn't going to be any trouble. You and Jeremy both worrying for nothing. We're just going to sing.

Jeremy walked in. He noticed Paul smoking.

Hey, man you don't smoke.

I do today. Got stuff on my mind, nothing to do with tonight.

Paul put his cigarette out in a cup.

Now, since you and Jeremy are nervous why don't you

two go hang out.

Did I say something like that? This place is so weird. Have you seen anyone like us?

I think I saw a few young dancers.

Come on, Jeremy we're singers not politicians. We do our show and go. Come on, Paul doesn't want us here.

Evita still flirted with Paul.

You need anything, Paul?

Paul smiled.

Just a good performance.

Evita and Jeremy walked out.

Paul got up and put on a pair of swim trunks. He put his feet in sandals and threw a towel over his back.

Chapter 26

Stage crew were sunbathing at the College Club beach. Some were swimming off a dock. Others threw a Frisbee. Mothers moved their toddlers to another side of the beach.

David and Lauren walked down to the dock where the SCOT was anchored.

Paul arrived and laid his beach towel out on the sand. Maggie, still reading under a tree, did not see Paul. Lauren spotted Maggie.

Oh, David, there's Maggie. Go get her. She ought to come with us.

David walked over to the bench.

Hi Maggie. Want to come sailing with us?

Maggie took a deep breath.

Come on, it will be good for all of us.

Okay.

Maggie closed her book. They walked down the dock to the SCOT.

Hey, Lauren greeted.

Lauren took the sails and tiller. Maggie and David climbed in. They sailed into the blue waters on a beautiful day. The wind was perfect. They embraced a perfect moment of silence on a sparkling blue lake. Then Lauren broke the silence.

Why don't you come to Seattle, David, you too Maggie?

Why this sudden interest in Seattle? We never traveled out there when Mom was alive.

That's just it, why not? Why didn't you ever come West?

And why didn't you ever come East, to Ithaca? Let's be honest, we came here because Mom was here. I'm just not drawn in that direction.

Oh, so now I'm just a direction?

Can we not do this? It's a beautiful day. Can't we just enjoy sailing?

There's lemonade and beer in the cooler, Maggie.

Lemonade.

David handed her a lemonade.

Here, David, you take the tiller, suggested Lauren.

Me?

You can do it I trust you.

Lauren, what are you thinking of? Neither of us are sailors.

David changed places with Lauren and took the tiller.

I'm not comfortable with this. Lauren we'll tip over.

Give me a chance, Maggie. David protested.

No, you've never taken a tiller. You don't even like video games.

I'm watching, Maggie. It's really okay.

Then I'm swimming back. She took her sundress off.

Lauren took the tiller from David. She did a quick 'ready about hard to lee' turn toward the shore.

Chautauqua After Hours

David could hardly believe it.
Maggie, are you crazy? Stay here.
Maggie plunged in.
She was glad she put her swimsuit on under her dress. Imagine giving David the tiller. As if he could steer his life or hers. Maggie did the freestyle over and over. She began to enjoy the water over her body. She could feel that her arms and legs were still strong even if she was 60. Thank God she had passed all her swimming tests at Girls' Club. She passed the tadpole test, the turtle and fish and advanced fish tests. She could still remember the swim from Girls' Club to the Bell Tower and the half hour of treading water when she felt like her legs would fall off. Splash. Splash. She had reached the little beach.
She felt a hand reach out to hers. He was there. Again. She took his hand and pulled herself to firm ground.
Young mothers on the beach watched the exchange.
Who is he?
I have no idea.
Who is she?
I think some older Chautauquan, lots of generations, you know.
Maggie was out of breath.
Here, my towel.
Maggie felt him place the towel around her shoulders. He was so quiet. His eyes so deep, deep, brown like a clear river of secrets.
Maggie took another deep breath.
Whew!
Take your time. That was quite a swim.

I'm just up the road. I really have to get out of this suit.
Lucky you didn't feel any seaweed around your legs.
Oh, I knew enough to skim the top.
He watched her breathing.
Oh, where are my manners? Thank you so much for the gladioli.
You're welcome.
Maggie kept looking at him. She wasn't sure why. She knew it was time now to leave and go back to the house and change. Their exchange was really over.
She handed him the towel.
I'm just up the road. Oh I said that.
She felt him watching her. She took a deep breath and began to speak the idea that had been swirling around somewhere in the dark water of her swim. It was rather like the seaweed. Was it too much? Too entangled to mention? Should she skim over her thoughts and not say anything to this man? God, what was the look behind his eyes? She dove under.
You know, we have this tradition at Chautauqua where we invite a performer home for dessert. Would you care to come?
I would.
Well, tomorrow night then around 8?
I'll be there if it's not too hard on you.
Oh, my Mother dying?
Yes, that and other things.
She knew what he meant.
You let me decide what I can handle here at Chautauqua.
All right.
8 o'clock. 33 James.
Maggie walked off.

Chapter 27

Maggie fixed a fruit salad in the kitchen. She held a small paring knife to cut the apples.
Lauren stood nearby.
You really should have given David a chance.
I didn't feel like capsizing.
I could have handled it.
Lauren, what are we talking about?
Okay, I know. But just remember Mom had a good life.
Maggie threw the paring knife into the sink.
Boy you never learn. The very same cliche again! Do you know what happens when we die? Does David? Nor do I! But I won't have you sum it up with some stupid cliche!
Maggie opened the wine cabinet. She pulled out a bottle, took a wine glass, her salad plate, and proceeded to the front porch. A car pulled up in front of the house.
Better not leave it there, you'll get a ticket.
A young man stepped out of the car.
Is this the Michaels' residence?
It is and you can pull the car into the driveway.
Chris Hare did as Maggie suggested. He stepped out of the car with his briefcase. Then he walked up the porch steps.

Mary Keating

Would you be Maggie Wood?
I am.
I'm Chris Hare. You called about some legal advice.
You're early. We said 3.
Sorry about that, should I leave?
Not at all. Would you like a glass of wine?
Oh, no, thank you. I have the papers.
My sister doesn't want the house and she is in the will to get it with me. My you're very young.
I graduated from Yale two years ago.
Well, can you do something about that?
The will?
Yes, the will.
Lauren walked to the porch.
Chris rose. Lauren and Chris shook hands.
Hi, I'm Chris Hare, the lawyer.
Hi, I'm Lauren, the troublemaker.
Lauren laughed. Chris laughed. Maggie didn't.
I told Chris you don't want the house, Maggie explained.
Correct, I live in Seattle so do by computer?
Sure, no problem. I can e-mail and attach the promissory note to you.
Great.
Maggie and Lauren looked at each other.
Gotta change, I'm late for tennis. Nice to meet you. Lauren went inside and up the stairs to her bedroom.

Chapter 28

Lauren passed by the guest room where David sat watching TV.

What? Too loud?

No, not to me. David, you can use Maggie's room again. The paint's dry if you want to lie down.

Sure, good idea.

Lauren walked into her bedroom. She lifted the sundress off her body and stood in her slip. David walked by at that moment. He noticed Lauren. She made eye contact with him.

When are you going for that drink with me? Lauren asked as she pulled her tennis shorts on.

I can't figure out when. You pick the time.

I'll let you know.

I think I'll stay in the guest room.

Oh? Suit yourself.

He walked along. Lauren finished dressing.

Chapter 29

Maggie rode her bike through the shadows of the street lamps. She parked her bike against a tree. The trees made a canopy above her as she stood undetected at the edge of the 'Amp'. She could pick out Paul on the stage. The orchestra quietly tuned up. The overture melody began softly resonating out into the empty space of the Amphitheater and beyond into the trees and night sky.

Paul stood with Evita at the half-stage mark. They were cued by the conductor. They walked toward the front of the stage. They softly introduced the story.

Then with their voices they each began their song. Evita sang *A Cockeyed Optimist*. Then Paul sang *Some Enchanted Evening*.

The conductor nodded 'yes', go on.

Maggie realized she was holding her breath and exhaled. One a.m. It was after hours. Most everyone was asleep at Chautauqua. All but the singers and Maggie.

Maggie walked her bike the fifty feet to the Backstage Cafe and left it under a bush. She walked inside and hid in the back corner. Weezie had several piles of cups on the counter. She brought the cups out to the tables. She noticed Maggie.

Chautauqua After Hours

Oh, Maggie I didn't see you come in. No Styrofoam tonight. My best.
Weezie smiled. Maggie smiled with her. Maggie put her elbows on the table.
Hell, I got the jitters and I'm not even in the show.
Maggie felt her own jitters coming on.
You know what Weezie? I just don't think I can stay tonight. I promise I'll be here opening night.
He's getting to you isn't he?
What do you mean? I just lost Mom I want to go home.
Okay, sorry, I'll see you tomorrow.

Chapter 30

A group of male teen-agers on bikes approached the Cafe as Maggie pulled her bike out of the bushes. She rode away. The boys threw their bikes down. They retrieved hidden paint cans near the foundation of the building. They took paint brushes, dipped them in black paint and wrote racial slurs on the front door of the Cafe. Then they rode off laughing into the dark.

Just thirty feet away the singers were crossing the red-brick walk on their way to the Cafe. They were chatting together. Evita and Jeremy walked side by side. They reached the front door of the Cafe and stopped cold. There were racial slurs bold as the sun.

I knew it, I knew it, Jeremy.

Evita cried. Where's Paul? Where's Paul?

Paul's not here, baby, he went to make his weekly phone call to Mississippi.

The conductor stepped forward and called 911.

Yes, we have a situation here, no one's hurt but you better come. The Backstage Cafe. Yes, officer.

Inside Weezie noticed the cast not opening the door. She opened the door and walked outside. She looked puzzled.

Chautauqua After Hours

They motioned to the door. Weezie turned and stared at the letters in paint.
    Oh, my god, no.
    The cast stood frozen. The police car pulled up.
Officer Biggs stepped out.
    Jimmy, I had no idea this was going on, Weezie blurted out.
    Call me Officer Biggs, Weezie, when I'm on duty.
    He walked to the door and put his hand on the paint.
    Fresh.
    So you all saw nothing?
    We just arrived after rehearsal, sir. The conductor spoke for the group.
    I see you are here again, Jeremy.
    Jeremy wanted to tell him where to shove it but he refrained.
    I just finished singing, sir.
    It must be that article in *The Daily*.
    Weezie kept staring at the front door.
    Well, I'm just going to clean it all off.
    Everyone knows about it. Biggs added again.
    Of course everyone knows about it. They read don't they?
    Weezie could see nothing but scrubbing would take care of the situation. Weezie ordered them away.
    Get on now, everyone go home. There's nothing to do here, Officer, go on. It's very late. But you better find out who did this, you hear me, Jimmy?
    Officer Biggs nodded his head and approached his car.
    The cast and conductor walked toward Bellinger.

Chapter 31

Maggie walked through the park. She felt a slight pain and tightening in her right shoulder and collapsed to the ground. Her mind hummed. She drew in deep breaths again and again.

God.

She put her fingers to her lips to try to get words out but nothing came. She stared.

Straight ahead she could see lights on in the living room. The smell of grass and flowers filled her nostrils. She lay quiet. The sky filled her brain. The stars spoke to her. For a brief moment she wanted to sleep under the stars.

Okay, okay.

She rolled herself upward. Slowly she grabbed the bench and stood up again. She took baby steps toward the porch.

Inside the house Lauren sat drinking a martini in her summer nightgown. It was opened sensuously. David sat in his summer pajamas holding a highball. Maggie opened the door.

I thought I was going to die.

What?

They both jumped up but not before Maggie viewed the

pajama party they seemed to be having.
　I collapsed right outside...in the park.
　You are out of breath. Here sit down.
　David tried to help Maggie into the living room. She didn't want to go.
　Do you want to go to the hospital?
　No.
　Did you fall off your bike?
　No, I just collapsed.
　Lauren handed her her drink.
　No, Lauren I don't want to drink! I just want to fall asleep for a long time. Sleep.
　Maggie shook her head and started up the stairs slowly.
　Lauren and David backed away.
　Get a good night's sleep and I'll make breakfast for the two of us, Maggie, a real married couple, sit-down breakfast.

Chapter 32

In the morning David fixed pancakes, bacon, and toast for himself. The coffee percolated.

Lauren walked in and sat down. David had on a new pair of running shoes.

Maggie isn't up yet?

No. Here you want some pancakes?

Oh, no this is your married breakfast, remember?

Lauren opened the front page of *The Daily*.

The story read:

Apparently teen-age boys could find nothing better to do last evening than smear racial slurs on the front door of the Backstage Cafe. Their racial slurs have since been removed by owner Weezie Horton. Suspects have been rounded up but no confessions have been obtained. Officer Biggs was on the scene shortly after Conductor Rogers called 911. The singers had just finished their after-hours rehearsal for South Pacific. If anyone has any information leading to the arrest of these teen-agers please notify the Chautauqua Police Department.

My God, do you think this is what had Maggie so upset, David?

Naw, I don't think she even knew about it. Hey take a

Chautauqua After Hours

look at my new sneakers. Want to come for a run?
 I'll just grab a piece of bacon. Better wait for Maggie.
 Lauren bit the bacon and smiled at David. David came over to her. He took the bacon away.
 You'll burn your tongue.
 Lauren rubbed her mouth with her fingers.
 See ya, David.

Chapter 33

Maggie entered the kitchen. No David. Nothing but dishes and leftover cold food.

Maggie turned the faucet on and began to do dishes. She noticed *The Daily* on the table. She sat down and read the article.

Oh, no.

Maggie couldn't stay any longer in the kitchen. Suddenly she was claustrophobic. She walked along the hallway to the door and grabbed a sweater, not caring if it was hot or cold outside. She walked toward the lake.

David stood at the kiosk looking at the photo of the cast of *South Pacific*. He had worked up a sweat running. As he looked Paul walked by on the red-brick walk. Other Chautauquans gathered on the red-brick walk headed for Bestor Plaza or the morning lecture at the Amphitheater.

David broke away and jogged toward the Backstage Cafe.

When he reached the front door he saw a man of color coming away from the front door. David did not realize it was Paul. They did not speak.

The door had a sign on it: CLOSED—BE BACK SOON.

David looked around for someone to show up. He didn't

Chautauqua After Hours

wait long before Weezie arrived.
Hey, David.
Hello, Weezie. You opening up?
Sure, come on in. That was some breach of Chautauqua etiquette last night.
Boys, teen-agers. What can you expect?
Well, come in, are you meeting Maggie here?
She was still sleeping.
David walked in behind Weezie. He took a seat after getting a coffee and donut.
Say David, I have brownies here for Maggie. Would you take them to her?
Sure, what a nice surprise! For dessert?
No, they're not for you but her guest.
David took the brownies from Weezie. He was puzzled.
Guest?
She told you then?
No, I'm not sure what you mean.
Lauren walked in the door.
Hi, Weezie.
Hi, Lauren.
Lauren moved close to David.
I'm just leaving.
Okay, what's that? Lauren pointed to the plate David held.
Brownies for Maggie's guest, explained David.
Sounds intriguing. What are we talking about?
Have no idea.
David and Lauren walked outside. They did not look at the scrubbed out letters on the door.
Oh, look at you David, you're sunburned on your nose.

Mary Keating

Am I?
Yes, right there.
She pointed to his nose with her finger.
They began to walk toward James Avenue.

Chapter 34

Maggie sat in her wicker chair on the porch reading her book. Lauren and David walked up the steps.
 Here's the dessert, Maggie.
 Weezie wouldn't tell us anything.
 Who is the guest?
 Well, it's my guest. What the hell! I've invited one of the singers to the porch tonight.
 David looked shocked.
 You remember, Lauren, the tradition?
 Not really.
 What tradition?
 Asking a performer to your porch for dessert.
 Lauren, did you see the rose of Sharon how it's bloomed?
 Maggie, it's pretty, responded David.
 Lauren?
 You don't have to point out something like that.
 What do you mean?
 I mean I can see. Just because I'm the baby doesn't mean I can't see.
 I was just sharing a moment with you.
 You were changing the subject.

Oh, go inside.
I intend to.
Lauren slammed the screen door. She yelled through the screen door.
How can you be married to her?
David took a seat.
Five miles today, Maggie. Shoes are great.
I don't think this is a good time to tell me this.
Sorry, I just couldn't see waking you again. I had to try the shoes.
And leave me with nothing but dishes to wash?
I blew it. So who's your guest?
Now who's changing the subject?
He's in *South Pacific*. Remember? I told you about the concert.
Do you know him?
I met him briefly at Weezie's but that's not the point; it's giving back to a performer.
Right. David thought for a long time.
He's black then?
His name is Paul. I'm not having that conversation with you.
What can Chautauqua be thinking?
What do you mean?
This diversity stuff won't work! Rogers and Hammerstein intended it a certain way.
My god, you're a racist!
That's what you think?
I do.
Forget it Maggie. You don't get to tell me that.

Chautauqua After Hours

Maggie wondered how she could get out of this conversation and still make her point.

I made quiche for dinner. After I cleaned up your breakfast mess.

It's summer Maggie, I know I messed up but I got all caught up in my new shoes. Like a kid I guess.

A kid, David? Please put the brownies on the dining room table.

David walked inside.

Chapter 35

Dinner was over.   The candles burned. Maggie got up and unwrapped the brownies. One was missing. Maggie looked at David.

Alright who ate a brownie?

Ah, Maggie it was just one. Look at all the rest of them here.

Lauren, what's the matter with you?

What's the matter with you?

David jumped into the fray.

We can go out and get another at the Cafe. If it's that important. But you don't eat dessert much anyway.

Maggie wanted to slap him.

David, when I want your opinion I'll ask for it.

I think I hate you Maggie, Lauren screamed.

Good! Then leave! Both of you! I have a guest coming and it's important to me.

David and Lauren left the table.

Maggie poured herself a whiskey and walked to the porch with the bottle. She sat down with her glass of Jameson. Maggie heard the soft whisper of the orchestra in the Amp playing classical music.

Chautauqua After Hours

She took another swig of Jameson. She looked out toward the park. There he was walking toward her. He crossed the street and slowly ascended the steps. He was in front of her. She stood and felt her fingers touch his wrist as they shook hands. She knew it was formal but she appreciated the gesture.

I want to thank you. It is very special to be here.
Are you hungry now?
Mind if I just sit here? Bellinger Hall dorms aren't built with porches.
He smiled. Maggie smiled.
Would you like a drink then?
Yes, what are you drinking?
Jameson.
The same please.

Maggie poured Paul a whiskey. She looked at his handsome face. Maggie suddenly felt time slow down. She was in no hurry with this night.

May I have a glass of water?
Oh, certainly, I'll be right back.

She walked to the kitchen. She grabbed a bottle of water from the refrigerator. She took it back to the porch.

He drank it like he was dying of thirst.

She watched his lips around the bottle. The way his head tilted back. His strong neck.

You live here all year?
Oh, no. It's my Mom's...well now my house. I live in Ithaca most of the year.
Are you enjoying Chautauqua?
Most of it. I think there are few people like myself,

though, he answered.
Yes, it's been this disturbing way for a long time.
I didn't think I'd run into the police here.
Oh, I am so sorry that happened.
There was a silence for an instant while the whole uncomfortable reality of the culture surrounded them.
Where are you from, Paul?
Mississippi. Singing got me out of there though.
Maybe I'll grow old here.
Old? Maggie you're still young. Why think old? You look young to me.
It's a shift. I guess now that Mom is gone and my sister is younger. Doesn't that mean I'm next?
No one can tell. Once I finish here I'm going home for my Mamma's 75th birthday party. Now that's older.
I tried giving my Mother a party. It didn't turn out too well.
Paul looked at Maggie in her grief.
He poured himself another drink.
Can I freshen yours?
Yes. I do have coffee and brownies inside.
I like it right here.
Does your wife travel with you...I mean...oh excuse me. That was wrong of me.
It's okay. She doesn't leave Mississippi. The South is home to her.
Look at the moon over there.
Paul looked. Then he took Maggie's hand.
He led her over to the park. They reached the bench where Maggie collapsed the night before. They both looked at the

moon, then sat down. There was a comfortable silence. Maggie broke it with her own thoughts.

David, that's my husband of twenty-seven years, works all the time...you would call him a workaholic. He used to love the cocktail parties I arranged for his clients, but now he goes out to fancy restaurants.

The moon moved around the tree and shone right on their faces.

You know just looking at the moon makes me forget North and South and all that business of the world. Just looking at you....Maggie.

Maggie laughed.

Oh, I just don't know where that came from. It's just this seems surreal to me.

It's okay; I think I understand. I haven't done this before either.

Maggie looked into his face. She wondered if she would like to be kissed.

Ho, ho, ho, ha ha ha, hee, hee, hee. Paul put his hand on his diaphragm. There I'm stretching my vocal cords.

William Faulkner said between grief and nothing give me grief.

Give me grief then, Paul answered quickly.

Coffee and dessert? Maggie asked.

Sure.

They walked back to the porch. Inside Paul noticed the piano right away.

Do you play?

No.

May I?

Of course.

Paul sat down. Maggie stood near him. She looked at his back. Paul noticed a picture of Ann Michaels.

Is this your Mamma?

Yes, when she was younger.

Any requests?

You pick. Maggie stood a little closer to the bench.

Paul began to play *Summertime*. He sang.

One of my favorites!

You're beautiful.

Maggie looked at Paul. David had not seen whatever Paul was seeing in her face for a very long, long, time. How could she feel like two different people at once?

Chapter 36

The College Club was filled with young people from various schools. They were not allowed to drink but often sneaked in a bottle or two of beer. Sometimes a flask of whiskey.

Lauren came through the grass toward the beach. David followed her. She lifted her sundress as she stepped into the small lapping waves of the lake.

Oh, what a night! Look at that moon.

Come on! I've got an idea!

She pulled David's hand and they entered the College Club up the stairs to the second floor where a mirror ball spun with the music.

Okay, now what?

We dance, come on. You know how to dance don't you?

Sure.

She pulled him onto the dance floor. Lauren moved her body to the music. David seemed awkward. He looked over the crowd.

Isn't that Hank?

Where?

David pointed. Lauren turned her head in the direction he

was pointing and there was Hank. She left David and walked quickly to Hank. Hank stood with a beer under his sweater. He was talking to another young man. He turned to see his Mother. Shocked, he tried to hide his beer.

Hank, what are you doing here? You're not old enough!

What are you doing here, Mom? You're not young enough!

Enough. You're leaving this minute. Take yourself home now.

Hank left the dance floor and walked toward the stairs and exit. He looked back to see Lauren talking to David who followed Lauren across the dance floor.

Come on I've had enough of the club.

Lauren and David left. Lauren dragged David by the hand to the beach again.

Okay this is a better idea; I guess that wasn't so great.

She began to strip off her dress. She stood in her underwear.

Come on David, we're going skinny-dipping before it gets too cold.

Are you crazy?!

No just ready to be spontaneous. Come on.

She took off her bra and panties and ran into the water.

Moments later David began to undress. He got down to his boxers. He took one look around to make sure Hank wasn't hiding in the bushes. Then he stripped and plunged in.

God this is ecstasy! I always dreamed of doing this. But I never got the nerve.

Lauren splashed David.

Stop. Stop. David smiled even though he asked Lauren

Chautauqua After Hours

to stop.

He splashed her back. He laughed a little. They both were silhouetted by the creamy moon rays on the water.

Lauren dove under and came back up.

Yuck. Too much seaweed down there...can't see a thing. We better go. Really.

Oh, party poop. Okay. It was fun though.

David started out of the lake to his clothes. He put them back on and shivered.

Lauren stepped out of the water. She leaned into David for a hug. His body was excited. Lauren noticed.

I'm dripping wet.

Okay, okay let's go get brownies at the Cafe.

No, I'm going back to the house and change. Maggie must be done with her 8 o'clock guest.

Okay.

Lauren took David's hand. They began to walk toward James Avenue along the lakefront.

Did you ever think we should have done it, David?

Us? I married your sister!

I mean sometime.

Oh, before I married Maggie?

Yeah, I mean I wanted to, sure.

I never thought about it really, answered David.

Oh, come on. You just didn't know it, replied Lauren.

Chapter 37

Maggie lay under the covers wondering why she was feeling sensations all over her body. She and Paul had not kissed. Yet the beauty of him playing the piano sent desire through her body. He had been so gracious. So gracious. What could she be thinking? What kind of death grip of mourning was this? Wasn't she in mourning? Her Mother gone. Her compass for life gone. No more words to hear ever again. No more peals of laughter.

The front door opened. She turned off her night light.

David and Lauren climbed the stairs. David walked into the guest room where he was still sleeping. Lauren walked into her bedroom. She changed into her nightgown, then tiptoed to the bathroom.

David was there first in his pajamas. He brushed his teeth. Lauren waited outside. David stepped from the bathroom and looked at Lauren. Lauren felt his eyes all over her.

She stepped toward him and felt his excitement. She touched him. He groaned. She touched him again. He kissed her.

They sneaked back to Lauren's bedroom. They fell into bed. David entered her.

Chautauqua After Hours

When Maggie heard nothing like a parting 'good night' from Lauren to David or David to Lauren, she decided to investigate. Maggie crept along the hallway and put her ear up against the door of the guest room. She could not hear her husband. She thought it odd he could be so still. Then she walked further down the hall to Lauren's bedroom. Sounds. More sounds. Sounds of muffled desire. Sounds of ecstasy from her husband and sister!

Maggie crept back to the guest room. She opened it and gathered up all of David's belongings and stuffed them in his small piece of luggage. She grabbed his Dopp-kit and luggage and stashed them in a garbage bag.

Maggie then walked down the stairs to the outside. She threw the bag but it landed in the garden.

No, no not there.

She picked it up and threw it again.

It went to the curb on the street.

Perfect. Maggie returned to bed.

Not long afterward David opened the door and returned to his bed. He turned the small light on and looked for his Dopp-kit. He stood there with his toothbrush in his hand and no Dopp-kit.

What?

David thought of no one but Maggie.

Maggie, I know you're awake. Open your door.

Maggie said nothing.

Where are my things?

Maggie said nothing.

Isn't this a bit childish? Okay well okay then....

David went down the stairs to the living room. He looked there and in the kitchen. He looked in the trashcan outside. He walked back through the house to the front door. He opened the door and stood on the porch. He saw the bag down by the curb.

Chapter 38

Maggie stood at the stove cooking breakfast. Coffee was percolating. *The Chautauquan Daily* sat on the table.

David sat at the table.

So are you going to talk or what?

Or what? Or what?

What do you mean? David asked.

What do you mean? You slept with my sister! Where the hell is she?

How should I know?

You knew last night! How could you? What is the matter with you?

I need a drink.

Oh, yeah maybe if you paid more attention to your wife you wouldn't need a drink.

I'm not allowed to pay attention to my wife. She doesn't even want me here.

And that gives you liberty to sleep with Lauren?

It was her idea. She has some crazy notion we should have done it years ago.

Oh I can believe that about my sister. Sounds like her.

But you? My husband falling hook, line, and balls.

Are you fixing me breakfast? I'm not going to get breakfast up at the diner. Look, Maggie, it was grief. Haven't you been saying grief does things to you?

Leave! And you're not even grieving so don't blame it on my Mother's death. Get out. Now!

Ah, Maggie there's got to be some kind of love there, after all we talk about Lauren all the time.

Are you crazy? Are you stoned? She raised her arms up and broke a dish in the sink with her fury.

David waited for a moment.

No, I'm just my boring accountant self, with nothing to say.

He came over to Maggie. She turned the spatula toward him.

Don't you come near me.

He backed up.

Lauren walked in.

Good. I want you to hear this, Lauren.

Maggie began to shake.

What? Lauren asked.

What? What? You just slept with my husband and you have the nerve to ask what? He's not your ex-husband. I want you to leave today, David, no this morning! Lauren and I have to figure out the will which is the only reason I can't kick her out but you, you need to go now.

I'm sorry, David, I told you she was crazy. Lauren poured coffee.

Crazy! Lauren, don't turn this on me. No one would believe this is our morning here at Chautauqua, while others

Chautauqua After Hours

go to hear someone with integrity and knowledge speak at the Amp.

People do odd things after death, isn't that what you believe Maggie?

I can't believe you are using Mom's death to rationalize your obsessive sex. Not to mention betrayal.

Maggie.

Go back to Ithaca, David.

Maggie was now in a complete meltdown. She stumbled to the chair.

Maggie, what is it? Lauren tried to help.

Don't touch me. You don't even want the house.

David put his hand on Maggie's shoulder. Then he left the room.

I want to talk about that. I've given it some more thought and something came to me. This can be Hank's after I die. I think Hank loves it here enough to want to come and it would mean another generation of Chautauquans.

Oh my God.

People can change their minds.

Lauren I can't talk with you right now.

The least you could do is get me a glass of water.

Lauren filled a glass of water. She handed it to Maggie.

There was a knock on the screen door.

Maggie are you in there?

Maggie!

Come in, Weezie. In the kitchen.

Weezie walked in and immediately sensed something was very wrong.

Are you okay, Maggie?

Just recovering.
Hey see you later.
Lauren darted out.
Recovering? What's happened?
It's hard to say the words.
Try.
Lauren and David slept together! Right here in my house! Last night!
Oh, my god, are they nuts?
I feel humiliated. I just threw David out.
And on top of that, Lauren now wants the house! How can the two of us ever be in this house now?
Well, you just come over and stay with me. She won't come that much.
Oh, she has reevaluated it all for my nephew.
I see. And David is gone?
He should be.
There was a long moment of empathy between friends. Weezie wanted to know about Paul.
Maggie, can I ask? How was the visit?
What visit? Oh, of course, Paul.
Did it go well?
He was a true gentleman and so polite. You know a kind stranger.
Maggie, it opens tonight. You better get your mind off this betrayal and see the show.
I know I wish...
You wish, what, Maggie?
Just...oh, nothing.

Chapter 39

Chaos surrounded the cast now standing in the hall. They stared at more racial slurs painted on the walls of Bellinger.

Officer Biggs stood near Paul. He interrogated him.

So you say you didn't see anything?

Nothing. I told you we take naps in the afternoon, Officer.

I see, well I have orders to paint the walls.

Biggs called on his cell.

Yes, get a goddamn ladder over here, George and lots of white paint.

Evita cried in Jeremy's arms. All the cast were talking and whispering.

Officer Biggs looked into the group with his eyes on no one in particular.

It will be taken care of quickly, he blurted out.

Not our walls, answered Jeremy.

Jeremy stared at Biggs. Paul gave Jeremy a look.

Well, I'll be going now I have to report this to the President.

Officer Biggs left.

Mary Keating

Paul motioned for the troupe to gather around him. He wanted to say a few words.

Tonight is opening night. We've worked and rehearsed for three weeks. Nothing is going to stop us from giving a good show—a great show. This 'silly season' stuff from teen-agers is none of our business. Put it out of your mind, they gotta deal with it in their own way. Who are we? We are performers, don't forget it. All right, break a leg.

The singers repeated the good luck expression.

Break a leg. They all hugged.

Paul walked into his dorm room. His cell rang.

Hello, Maggie is that you?

I just wanted to wish you a wonderful opening night. Should I say 'break a leg'?

Sure. Thank you.

Is anything wrong?

No, all good.

I'll be sitting in the front row.

I'll look for you. Good-bye.

Good-bye.

Chapter 40

Maggie wrapped a shawl around her shoulders and walked down the hall past Lauren's room. She left the house and started through the park to the Amphitheater.

Sounds of excitement penetrated the air. People were gathering on the long benches. The seats were filling up. The orchestra members came on stage. There was applause.

Maggie got to her front row bench. She slid in and settled down with her eyes glued to the front of the stage. She could hardly believe she made it there given such a huge betrayal. She knew her strength was hiding somewhere underground. Whatever consequences she would have to face with both David and Lauren, it could wait. Right now, in the moment of a Chautauqua summer night, at a special concert of her favorite musical, she would bear the pain. For one night of musical pleasure she would keep her hurt and rage under control. She had to. There was Paul.

Then something unexpected took place.

Paul came to the front microphone and began to speak.

Before we begin with our performance of *South Pacific* I want to say a few words. There's a reason we are here. Foundations in New York City funded the money to hire us; to hire persons of diversity. It's a look backwards and forward through Rogers and Hammerstein's *South Pacific* and the messages in the show. When are we going to learn? Right here at your Chautauqua there's racism. Right there on your front porches we find total exclusion. This isn't Hollywood. This is the American experience of Chautauqua.

A member of the audience yelled 'get on with the show.'

Sure I hear you brother. You want us to sing.

The orchestra began to softly play the overture.

You show us you can talk to us. You show us you want to hear this beautiful music no matter what color our skin.

Maggie stood up and clapped. Row by row each part of the audience stood up and clapped.

Paul watched.

Thank you.

At 8:12 p.m. the orchestra began the overture. The audience broke into a roar of clapping and whistling. Maggie's face glowed. The concert continued with all the songs. Paul stepped forward and sang *Some Enchanted Evening*.

Maggie could feel tears on her cheeks. The concert ended. More clapping; a standing ovation. Maggie couldn't move. She sat while 4,000 audience members walked out of the Amphitheater.

Within five minutes Paul walked quietly toward Maggie. He took her shawl which she had let drop off her shoulders and put it back on her body. He was quiet. She looked into his eyes. She wondered if she had perspiration on her face. It had been such a rousing night. He took her hand so gently without a word.

She walked with him. He paused. He stepped toward the

Chautauqua After Hours

Amp's stage floor. She followed him. Though there were no stage lights on she was not afraid of falling. He embraced her in a dance. They danced across the wide wooden floor. She moved into his soul without knowing just where it would take her.

She couldn't understand where his fountain of energy came from. Wasn't he exhausted? Or was she just projecting her own fatigue from the day which would soon come back into her reality? She wanted to keep it out now and dance. So she did.

They walked off the stage and up the steep ramp to the red-brick walk and then a right turn up James. When they got to the house Paul stopped. Before stepping up to the porch he spoke.

We can help each other.

They stood in darkness under the large maple. She wanted to hear him go on and on with whatever words he wanted to speak.

His words, she thought. Tender. Kind. She was ready to answer.

Yes, we can.

She had given him words. Agreement. Possibility. Given herself hope. Not the morning anger. She wanted to hear his voice again and again.

You love this house, don't you?

Oh yes. Very much.

Would you ever think about a trip away?

A trip?

I've got my ticket to Mississippi for that birthday party I told you about. For my Mamma. I'll buy you one.

That is if you'll come.

Mississippi?

I know you've got a picture of the South...who doesn't from all our history? But it's better now; poor but better.

You don't have to assure me, Paul.

Yeah, well, another ticket then? My Mamma would love to meet you and she makes the best biscuits in the state.

Maggie heard the invitation in a distant place in her heart. She watched her feet so as not to stumble going up the steps. He followed her.

Maggie. I'm sorry I've been going on about my roots. I don't know why. What?

It's just that it's hard to realize the man you married has betrayed you. And here you are sounding so pure and true to my ears. A total stranger.

I've always depended on the kindness...

In unison they both answered—

Of strangers.

They both laughed knowing they had just completed the line from *A Streetcar Named Desire*.

The porch light was off. They looked at each other. Paul's hands moved up Maggie's arms to her neck. They moved closer and closer to each other. Maggie was happy to feel the space of the porch and night and Paul not crowding her.

He bent down and kissed her lips. Her tongue met his. He kissed her again and again. She pulled back.

Do you want me to go?

I'll come with you, Paul.

Maggie released her body from his. He smiled with her

news. She opened the door and walked inside. He jumped the four steps in joy.

Chapter 41

At one a.m. Maggie walked upstairs to crawl into bed with warm delicious thoughts of Paul. She could walk the hall blindfolded for she knew every creak in the floor, every light switch on the wall. She knew Lauren was watching TV in the guest room now that David had left. She wondered why Lauren never read. Maggie knew she would not be able to avoid passing the guest room on the way to the bathroom.

Maggie started for the bathroom door without stopping.
Maggie?
Lauren jumped up and came to the hall.
Maggie can you forgive me?
Maggie knew Lauren was going to insist that they get along again and that this situation with David should be shoved under the rug or just forgotten. Lauren had a way of shoving everything under the rug.

Maggie wasn't sure what she could do about it anyway. It had happened. The husband who could not make it to her Mother's funeral had slept with her sister. It had moved Maggie's reality along at lightning speed. Her Mother's death had moved her brain cells to a place where she couldn't analyze life as well as she used to. Could she ever forget what her sister had done?

You were acting so horrible.

Stop.

I don't want David and he doesn't want me. He's...he's a workaholic.

I know that. We are never going to have the same relationship again—you and I.

Maggie, please forgive me, you can forgive, I know you can.

Maggie wasn't sure about that. Yet she didn't want to fill up the night thinking about David and Lauren. She needed her space back, the space she felt on the porch with Paul. She wanted to crawl into her nightgown and lay down in her bed.

Go to sleep, Lauren. I'm tired.

All right. Okay. I'm leaving again for Seattle. Hank and I will be back in two weeks for the regatta.

I'm leaving too.

You are, where?

Mississippi.

Oh, that's just up the road. What do you mean?

With Paul.

Do you know him well enough?

Probably not.

Be careful. He's married.

Ah, married, like David is to me?

Maggie watched Lauren's face wince.

I suppose there's a reason for Mississippi?

His Mamma's 75th birthday party.

Lauren got it. She looked at Maggie and for the first time

since their Mother had died they looked at each other with true empathy.

Then go.

I will. Now, good night.

Lauren went back to the TV. Maggie went into the bathroom and brushed her hair. She looked in the mirror. She couldn't place the face that stared back at her. She took her shower and then she grabbed the bathrobe from a hook and wrapped it around her. She stepped into the hall.

Maggie opened the door to her bedroom ready to remember Paul's face and kisses. Instead there was David. David lay naked on the bed! He held a bottle of whiskey.

What the hell? David? I told you to get out of my house! You've startled me...put your clothes on.

I got here a few hours ago.

You mean Lauren knows you're here?

No, I was real quiet. She's watching TV.

He poured a glass for Maggie.

No, David. I said get some clothes on.

He got off the bed. He grabbed his boxers and trousers.

I don't want to drink. What can you be thinking?

You brought me to this.

I did? Come on. Who slept with my sister?

Who never showed any passion for me?

What? I'm not having this conversation now. We are going to separate. I'll get a lawyer.

You walled me out as much as I did you.

Fine, have it your way. Now leave and don't let me find you sneaking in here again.

Come home, Maggie come back to Ithaca.

Chautauqua After Hours

And walk around in an empty house? Never. You need to decide about Lauren by yourself in Ithaca. Are you going to marry her?

What? You can't be serious. It meant nothing.

Why is that always the line? I'm going to bed and you are getting a room in a hotel or B and B.

He came toward Maggie.

Please Maggie, can't we work this out? Twenty-seven years together can't go away because of one night. Give me a break, honey. Work with me.

David, it's over. Really. Over. Now go.

He stood back in shock. He grabbed his shirt and jacket, shoved his bare feet in his loafers and walked to the door. With his hand on the door knob he turned to look at Maggie.

Good-bye David, my lawyer will be in touch.

He left and closed the door. Maggie stepped to the second-floor porch. She watched him walk toward the hotel across the park. She felt relief.

Chapter 42

An hour later Paul opened the windows for air. The heat was oppressive and the room's air-conditioner was broken. His cell phone rang. He looked for it under a pile of clothes. He stood in a towel after his shower.
Damn.
He picked up the cell phone.
Hello.
Paul, hello.
Maggie, anything wrong?
No, did I wake you?
No, couldn't sleep.
Me either. I just called to say hello.
You haven't changed your mind?
No.
I'm happy you called. I'll pick you up in fourteen hours.
I'll be here. Night.

Chapter 43

The next afternoon Chris Hare waited for Lauren on the porch. Lauren stepped outside.

Good morning, I understand you don't want a promissory note.

I'm so sorry I was just stupid to not see this is a house for my son too.

Not to worry, lots of people get confused with wills. It's an emotional time.

Would you like to see a photo of my Mother?

Sure, I cleared out my morning. They walked inside.

Lauren showed him a photo from the top of the piano.

Maggie walked in.

There we are on a trip to Biloxi, Mississippi. Mississippi, Maggie.

Yeah, oh right.

Anyway we were all singing and dancing. Dancing to *Dixie* I think. Little Northern girls.

You both look real happy, Chris observed.

I have to pack. We're good now, Chris, all changes made?

All good.

Maggie lingered.

Lauren's eyes faded into Chris's. She felt her mind go away for a moment. She was in Biloxi, Mississippi. Two sweet girls in pinafore dresses were sitting at a table with white tablecloths and favors. Musicians played *Dixie*. Her Mother danced with her father. Lauren, eight and Maggie, twelve ate ice-cream sundaes.

The grown-ups formed a conga line. Her Mother came over and took her daughters' hands. She led them onto the dance floor. Maggie danced behind her Mother and Lauren held onto Maggie's hips. They snaked around the room spinning with delight.

Are you all right? Chris asked.

Yes, just remembering something.

Lauren stood up and took Chris's hands.

Come on.

What?

Come on, Maggie.

"I wish I lived in Dixie, away away, I wish I lived in Dixie..."

Lauren pulled Maggie out of her seat. Maggie surprised herself by joining in. She remembered the time with her Mother in front in the conga line. Maggie held onto Chris's hips and Chris held onto Lauren's. They snaked around the living room to the dining room to the hallway. As they passed the piano Maggie let go abruptly. Lauren and Chris both stopped.

No I'm not going to do this. You don't get to pull me into some memory, Lauren. I'm going to pack.

Maggie walked upstairs.

Chapter 44

At 3:45 p.m. Maggie sat ready on the porch with her bag next to her. She sipped from a water bottle. Three minutes passed. She walked to the garden and plucked a few dead leaves off the geraniums. She sat back down on the porch.

No Paul. Four o'clock.

Jenny, the next-door neighbor and friend of Ann Michaels, walked through the park.

Hello, Maggie.

Hi, Jenny.

I sure will miss my talks with your Mother come September.

I know, she loved getting together then.

Jenny continued toward her home on upper James.

Maggie walked back into the house. Now she put her hand in front of her mouth to keep her angst from gushing out in a cry.

Chapter 45

At Bellinger, one could still see the words whitewashed and sloppily painted. In the dining room, the singers were drinking and dancing while Soul and Hip-Hop music played. Evita and Jeremy danced together. A few joints of marijuana were passed around. Paul walked around giving out hugs and kisses. He carried his water bottle and drank in-between good-byes. Evita threw her arms around Paul.
　See you in Buffalo.
　You bet.
　Police cars and a limousine pulled up. The chauffeur opened the door. The President of Chautauqua stepped out. He walked with Officer Biggs to Bellinger. Paul walked toward the front door. He saw Officer Biggs. Paul looked at his watch. The President approached him. They all stood right where the sloppy paint covered the racial slurs.
　Excuse me, aren't you one of the singers? The President asked.
　Yes, sir. Paul answered.
　I wonder if you can help me.
　I'm really through here.
　The President came close.

Chautauqua After Hours

It will only take a moment. Who did it? Who did it?
As I explained to Officer Biggs it happened during the afternoon when we were all resting...no one saw a thing.
Is that your room? You mean you didn't hear anything?
I'm a heavy sleeper.
You're telling the truth?
Excuse me why would I lie?
I see. Well best be going then. You can't help us here.
Paul was incredulous.
I really expected more from this place. Maybe you ought to look at what is going on here.
I'll take care of Chautauqua. We'll get this sorted out. Officer Biggs you need to order another coat of paint.
Paul walked outside and stood stunned in the twilight. He was late. He hurried to the parking lot to get his rental car. He threw his bags inside, turned the ignition on and drove toward James Avenue.

Chapter 46

Maggie was sitting in the kitchen. She had the bottle of Jameson on the table. She sipped from her favorite cup. She heard thunder. She looked at the clock on the wall. 5:30 p.m. So late, what could it be? She had called Paul's cell but it was busy or not even on. She did not leave a message.

When she looked up there he was gliding up to the screen door without a rain jacket. He tried the door. It was locked. Though Maggie never locked the door during the day.

Maggie, may I come in?

I can't go, Paul. Please understand.

I got held up. I'm so sorry. Let me explain.

I'm tired of explanations. Please don't.

Something happened; I couldn't get away.

Paul, you go to your Mamma's party and I'll stay here. It wasn't a good idea anyway.

Come to the door, Maggie.

Maggie started toward the door holding her cup of whiskey. Then she stopped.

Maggie, it's me Paul.

I can't do it.

Yes, you can.

Chautauqua After Hours

Maggie took another baby step.
What's happened, Maggie?
Maggie covered her face. The angst she was trying to keep away rose up in a cry.
What is it?
I've lost my bearings.
Maggie come.
Go Paul, I want you to go.
He was drenched in the rain. Yet he seemed to glow in the drops coming from his face. Maggie closed the door. He was shut out. She waited in silence. He didn't say another word. She called out his name softly just one time. She heard the car start up. It thundered again. She was cold. She turned back to the living room and placed an old 33 on the record player. This was her moment to understand what her life was coming to. What did she want? The age-old questions floated around the rooms of her Mother's home. Now hers.

Chapter 47

The bayous and gulf formed a sultry environment. Cotton Shores, Mississippi sat near a small inlet. A small tan bungalow, in need of a coat of paint, was lit up and festive. Oatgrass blew. Cajun music played. Paul walked happily toward the front door.

His Mamma, Mrs. Rains, sat inside the living room in a big stuffed chair. The dining table was filled with cooked greens from all the gardens in the neighborhood. Chicken. Potatoes. Macaroni and cheese. A big pot of crayfish simmered on the kitchen stove. Friends gathered around Mamma. There was a cake with 75 candles placed on the card table next to her. Mamma bubbled as she opened presents. When she looked up from the ribbons she saw Paul.

Give your Mamma a big kiss. Paul leaned over and kissed his Mamma.

An uncle picked up the cake.

It's time to blow out the candles...you...got's here just in time, Paul.

Oh we've got to sing first. Paul started the room off with *Happy Birthday*.

"Happy Birthday to you, happy birthday to you happy

Chautauqua After Hours

birthday dear Mamma happy birthday to you".
    Mamma took a deep breath and blew out sixty candles. Fifteen remained behind. Friends all leaned in toward the cake. Paul blew out the last candles. A big roar of happiness went up in the room.
    Mamma you got so much stuff what ya going to do with it all?
    Gives it out again for Christmas presents.
    All her friends laughed.
    Paul walked into his first floor bedroom and tossed his bag on the bed. He took his shoes off. He sat down. He looked at his cell phone and thought about calling Maggie. He put the cell on the nightstand. Paul looked at a photo of his wife when they were first married. Paul turned the picture face down.
    He got undressed and laid down on his pillow. He hummed a few bars of *This Nearly Was Mine.*

Chapter 48

When Paul walked into the kitchen in the early morning light he saw his Mamma cooking up biscuits. His Mamma watched him. He tried to get Maggie on the cell. No answer. He covered his mouth and left a message. He carried his shoes.

Maggie, I just want to say...it's all good.
Come sit down son, these biscuits 'bout done.
Paul sat down. He puts his shoes under the table.
Oh, do they smell good.
Mamma took the biscuits out of the oven. She brought the pan over to Paul.
Don't burn your fingers.
She used a knife to release two biscuits for Paul.
Eat.
Paul slathered the biscuits with butter. Mamma brought him bacon and eggs. Paul drank nearly a pitcher of water.
Is my divorce legal?
Papers just come yesterday. You wanna' read them?
Sure do.
Mamma got the papers out of the cupboard. She handed them to Paul. He read them.

Chautauqua After Hours

Mamma stood behind Paul and touched his head and hair.
It's been rough, ain't it baby?
I'm free, Mamma.
You remember, you done no wrong. Now you can make life better. Remember how we talk? Now you can sing anywhere. No ties back here in this backwater.
Ties to you Mamma.
Paul put his arms around his Mamma. They held each other. Silence.
Mamma, I met someone.
I thought you actin' like you gots sometin' to tell your Mamma. Honey, she good for ya?
I think she is. I sure hope she is. We just met a few weeks ago at Chautauqua.
Chatta—qua, what's that funny name?
It's a big gated place in New York. I sang there.
Well, if you sings there, it must be good.
Paul bent around his chair looking for his shoes. His Mamma handed them to him.
Your Mamma still good for her boy.
Mamma, I have to leave.
Mamma handed him a bag of biscuits.
You take 'em on the plane. Give one to your girl. You be happy Paul, you gone from here now. My boy gots a beautiful voice.
Paul hugged and kissed his Mamma.

Chapter 49

Maggie and Weezie sat on the porch at 33 James Avenue. They drank wine and nibbled on hors d'oeuvres.
I don't know. He wanted me to go home with him. Maybe I should have.
You're right maybe you should have.
What?
You know I won't say anything about it. I only know him as a customer. You're someone special, didn't he let you know you're special?
Maggie sat quietly. She thought of Paul. How he touched her darkness. How he lit up her mind. How he kissed her mouth. Maggie heard her own long silence. She came back to Weezie's question.
He did make me feel special.
Maggie watched a car pull up into the driveway. Lauren stepped out first. Hank climbed out and went to the trunk for their bags.
Hank and Maggie embraced. Hank gave Weezie a big hug. Maggie and Lauren kept their distance and did not embrace.
Weezie spoke first.

Chautauqua After Hours

Well, look what the cat dragged in. Aren't you a few days early?
What do you mean, Weezie?
Maggie said the day after tomorrow.
Well, I sent a postcard. Didn't you get it, Maggie?
Can't remember. Maggie looked coldly at Lauren.
Weezie walked down the steps.
I'll see you later, Maggie.
Okay.
Come on Hank, let's unpack. Lauren put her arm around her son.
They walked inside leaving Maggie on the porch. She wondered what form her anger and feelings of betrayal would take during this new visit from Lauren? Could she just forget such an infraction of rules? The marriage contract? The culture's morality of right and wrong?
Hank appeared first in his sailing duds.
Maggie the race is in three days...will you come? I can get you a front row seat.
Count me in.
Great.
Maggie loved Hank. That made it harder to stay angry. Still your own sister in bed with your very own husband. What had that been like for each of them? Did they stop in the middle and talk about her? Did David compare? It was all sick and she wondered how often this thing happened. Why did she have to be the first in her circle of friends to be in this mess? No one had ever talked about this situation in all the lunches at the library in Ithaca where she worked. She kept feeling like taking long cold showers smothering herself

with fragrances like lavender, lemon balm and roses. Keeping her head under the water was the best thing in the world to keep her from her own pain. Then there was Paul to think about. Paul had not seen her as an angry woman. Paul. Tenderness. Kindness. Remember those words.

Lauren walked onto the porch.

I'm going down to the docks. We're doing our last practice.

Maggie nodded and let Lauren go.

Chapter 50

Two days later was a brilliant blue Saturday. The docks were filled with SCOTs. Lauren and Hank untied the ropes and lifted the anchor. All the sailors did the same. Maggie sat in a front row seat in her folding chair. She looked through binoculars. She waved to Hank.

The race began. The sails lifted. The flying SCOTs sailed out into the lake and began the course around the buoys. Maggie thought Hank and Lauren were in second place. They sailed, a wind came up, they burst ahead. Hank was at the tiller.

Maggie jumped up and cheered wildly.

Come on Hank, come on. Go. Go.

Hank and Lauren sailed around the last buoy and won the race.

Yahoo. He did it, yes.

Maggie was still jumping up and down when a young woman stopped by. The young woman was eating an ice-cream cone.

Is he your son?

No my nephew. He won.

Maggie looked more closely at the woman.

Mary Keating

Oh my, aren't you from *South Pacific*? I thought everyone left.

I'm Evita. I just wanted to feel the place a little on my own. Do you come here every summer?

I do.

You're so lucky. It's beautiful.

It is...so where do you go next?

Oh, not sure. The director's going to talk to all of us in Buffalo. We never know. Not 'til he tells us.

I see.

See ya.

Evita walked off.

Maggie ran up to Hank as he came toward her. Hank was waving a check.

One thousand dollars, Maggie.

You're kidding?

Nope. It's great.

You were great. Your Grandma would be so proud. I'm so proud.

Maggie and Hank hugged.

Listen, you must be hungry, Hank, let's go back to the house and I'll fix us something to eat. And a bottle of champagne. I think this deserves a bottle of champagne.

I'm starved! Aren't you Mom? Hank asked.

I am, answered Lauren quietly.

They all started to walk on South Lake Drive toward James Avenue. Maggie's thoughts were now on her conversation with the young actress. She wondered what the meeting in Buffalo would bring. Would Paul come back to her after she sent him off that day in the rain? He had called and said

Chautauqua After Hours

'it's all good'. Maggie hoped that was enough and that he would come to the house after Buffalo. She had to hide her feelings from Lauren. Lauren did not deserve to come into Maggie's private world. Lauren dangled somewhere outside the sister bond now.

Now she must think of dinner. Steak tonight, though most of the time she ate like a vegetarian. She was starving. Steak and potatoes, she knew Hank would appreciate a meal like that.

Chapter 51

The years of fundraising were about to effect everyone's lives once more. The cast all sat down in Buffalo's Shea's Theater, where they thought they would play next. Excitement filled the air.

Jeremy and Evita sat next to each other. Paul stood on the side.

The director leaned against the stage. There was a hush.

Now I know you all think this is our next theater but it's not. Toronto isn't next either.

He took a deep breath. There was a hush.

Our patrons got together after Chautauqua and decided we are good enough to go to Europe and play there. We are on our way to Paris then London. They came up with this rather quickly.

Squeals of happiness.

Paul felt a slight tightening of his throat.

How long will we be out of the country? Paul asked.

The director looked over the whole cast and took a moment.

Yes, the most obvious question, Paul. We are going to be away for two to three years. It's a very big deal to have our

Chautauqua After Hours

backers believe in this show and take the risk. I hope all of you will stay but as you know you can leave. Your contract allows it. But think about it.
Audiences in Europe will love us.
Paul shook his head. He realized how few hours he had left in America.
Okay talk it over. If you have any more questions come up and ask. Then you better call your loved ones. We will fly from here to New York and then to Paris tomorrow night, explained the director.
Paul rushed outside to his car. He threw his bag inside and sped away down Route 90 to exit #60 at Westfield, New York.

Chapter 52

Maggie poured a round of champagne for Hank and Lauren. She felt relaxed with her feet out of her flats under the table. It had been a good celebration with Hank. Hank ate it all.

It was delicious, Aunt Maggie.

Thank you, you're old enough for champagne tonight, Hank. Maggie filled his glass. She let Lauren fill her own.

Hank proposed a toast.

To Mom, my first mate.

Maggie raised her champagne flute. Lauren smiled at Hank.

Want to go for a sail with me tomorrow, Aunt Maggie?

Sure, I'd love it.

There was a knock at the door.

Is that you Weezie, we're in the dining room. Come on in.

There was another knock. Lauren looked at Maggie. Maggie shoved her feet back into her flats and got up to answer the door. When she opened the door there was Paul. Maggie fell back a step with surprise. She opened the screen door.

Come in, are you all right?

Chautauqua After Hours

I just drove from Buffalo. Fast.
Buffalo, I see.
Lauren and Hank walked toward the hallway where Paul and Maggie stood.
We're celebrating Hank's regatta win. This is my nephew Hank, this is Paul Rains.
Nice to meet you, congratulations, Paul replied.
Thanks. Do you sail?
No, I'm afraid not, answered Paul.
I'm taking Aunt Maggie out tomorrow.
Lauren felt the need to disappear.
This is Lauren, my sister.
Hello.
We've had a long day, please excuse us, Lauren replied.
Hank and Lauren walked upstairs.
Paul took off his jacket and Maggie hung it up.
Come into the living room.
They walked in.
You didn't answer my call.
I know, replied Maggie.
I didn't think I'd see you again.
Why?
I wasn't very kind sending you away in the rain.
You did what you had to do, Maggie.
He turned away from her and looked out the curtained window. Maggie walked to the dining room to get another champagne glass. She poured a glass for Paul. She re-entered the living room. Paul stood by the window.
What is it, Paul? She handed him the glass of champagne.

Mary Keating

Thank you. All right here it is...the director just made his announcement to us all in Buffalo. It was a hush-hush meeting.

Maggie looked over his handsome face again. Now he had a small beard stubble. She wondered what it would be like to wash and trim his hair. To feel him sitting in front of her with his back against her breasts. She had visualized his face a thousand times since the night he left in the rain.

She couldn't believe she was getting another chance to be with him. She thought she could hear his voice but that was just her own imagination. She was so grateful they were not young and foolish or else this meeting would never have happened. They would have separated and never given each other another chance. Maggie felt the miracle of another chance happening in the very breath she took. Did Paul hear her thoughts?

Go on.

My Mamma told me the roots is a powerful thing but somewhere it got lost with me. I like to go places and sing.

What did the director say? Please, sit down.

He sat on the couch. He placed his champagne glass on the coffee table. He looked at Maggie.

I heard what the director said. Loud and clear. I got all pulled up in my chest and had to come here right away. To your door. You're the one I had to see...do you understand?

Maggie could only think that he was not remembering his wife when he got the news he was about to share. She could feel the breeze from the open window come into the room. It moved through the room and out again across Chautauqua and the cool evening.

Chautauqua After Hours

Paul, what are you trying to say?
Everything's good. It's better than I ever dreamed it could be. Than I deserve.
You deserve everything.
He surrendered to his new reality and looked deep into her face.
We're not going to Toronto or Buffalo, the patrons have arranged for us to go to Paris and then London.
Then he added:
For two or three years.
Maggie couldn't hear two or three years right now as anything that meant 730 days or 1095 days of minutes, seconds, and hours, passing and passing with each sunrise then day and each sunset then long night. No two or three years sounded more like two or three weeks in her mind. It was short. Paul would be right back.
Two to three years....really?
Paris, la vie en rose, jazz, blues, the city of light.
Oh, dear she could hear his excitement. His voice stopped. He held out his hand. Maggie let him take hers.
I'm not sure what this means. What does this mean, Paul?
I'm not sure either. What do you think?
I think you've been given a chance that comes only once.
My life is singing.
At this moment I'm not sure what my life is. My God, two or three years.
I know.
Did you expect me to go with you? To be your woman in Paris?
Just let me know I can be your man.

We just met.
Sometimes it happens. I'm saying you and I understand each other. Don't you feel it?
Maggie closed her eyes.
He stood up. He pulled her to him. There she was again pressed against his comforting chest.
What do you see?
Nothing. Dark swirls.
He held her head and face.
Imagine the lights of Paris. Us in Paris together. You and me. Free. Can you hear the music? We could get married. Our life could begin again.
He kissed her. She felt her own darkness blend into his light. He moved his mouth around hers. She thought she heard the word married but she wasn't sure.
It's crazy crazy, I'm too old.
You're not! You're a beautiful woman who gives me something no woman ever has. I can't just leave that...throw my heart away you wouldn't want me to would you? What I'm saying is I've fallen in love with you!
For the first time in Maggie's life she was without words. But under the deep silence she was completely trusting of the moment that the universe had just given her. She believed Paul.
He pulled away from Maggie. Maggie's mind did a quick broad jump in thought and suddenly she was caught in minutiae.
I don't even speak French. Where do we sleep?
What?
Do we sleep in bunkbeds like at Bellinger?

Chautauqua After Hours

Anywhere we find usually near the theater.
Paul looked deep into Maggie's face. He waited. Then.
It's a fine house, here, Maggie, but Paris? I'm parched, may I have a glass of water?
Maggie was happy for the chance to break away. She walked to the kitchen and poured Paul a glass of water. From the kitchen she called to him.
When do you leave?
Tomorrow.
Maggie walked back to Paul who had moved from the living room to the piano. He sat at the keys. Maggie handed him the water. He drank quickly. She hoped he would not play something that would melt her heart again.
But he didn't. So with the silence of the piano and the memory of his beautiful playing of songs she sat down and cried on his shoulder.
Don't you weep no more, Maggie.
He took her in his arms. They both rose from the piano bench. He walked slowly up the stairs with Maggie behind him. When they got to the second floor Maggie guided Paul into her bedroom.
Maggie looked around quickly hoping her husband was not there again to surprise her. He was not.
Paul began to undress Maggie. Maggie unbuttoned his shirt. They took their time...one piece of clothing after another. Then the passion exploded on the sheets.
Later, after making love Maggie rested her head on Paul's shoulder. It was 3 a.m. The Bell Tower gongs filled the air, one, two, three.
Will you come, Maggie?

Kiss me, Paul.
I have to leave at 6 a.m.
Then we have three more hours.
They began to make love again. Maggie listened to the house after they finished. She wondered if Lauren had heard this fusion of bodies meeting in darkness? She knew Hank was a heavy sleeper and wouldn't wake. Paul drifted into a short sleep.
And there she was feeling the pure beauty of the world. Fragile and awake with this stranger who gave her a feeling of rapture in her own soul. She was amazed by the mystery of it all unfolding in her own Mother's home.
Sounds, smells, touching fingers and hands, bodies over and under, two new faces looking deep into each other's eyes. Was any of this real? Where had Maggie gone to be doing this? Why weren't her old familiar patterns and parameters helping her now? She watched the clock move from 5 a.m. to 5:01 to 5:02 to 5:03 to 5:04 then Paul stirred.
What time is it?
5:05. Would you like me to walk you to the door?
No, thank you. I've got to go.
I know.
He dressed and walked down the stairs quiet as a cat. He opened and shut the front door then the screen door. Then he was gone.

Chapter 53

Five hours later she could hear the refrains of *Holy, Holy, Holy* from the Amphitheater. The choir was singing for the Sunday church service. An airport in Buffalo, an airport in New York City, the City of Light...Paris. So far away. She touched the sheets. She had trouble lifting her body from their warmth. Something had shifted inside her being and she didn't want to disturb it by getting out of the bed.

Finally all the minutiae began. Bed made. Shower and dressing and filling the washer with a pile of clothes. A cup of coffee. And calling Weezie. She opened the windows.

She walked out on the second-floor porch. Sunday morning at Chautauqua kicked in: the freshness, the morning service in the Amphitheater, Chautauquans walking from other religious houses on the red-brick walk. The Bell Tower sounding its chimes at noon. Gong, gong, gong, gong, gong, gong, gong, gong, gong, gong, gong, gong. Twelve gongs. Then *God Bless America* was heard all over the grounds.

Weezie how about some shopping today? Great. I'll walk over in fifteen.

Maggie walked across the park. Lauren and Hank walked toward her from the Amphitheater church service.

Hank hugged Maggie.
Come see us sometime, Aunt Maggie.
Hank left for the house and packing up.
Well, today's the day. Back home. We're still sisters?
Genetically that's true.
Well can I ask?
You may, but I probably won't tell you anything.
Do you want him?

Maggie was surprised with the question but she had to admit it did show some intuition on her sister's part. She knew that Lauren might have heard Paul in Maggie's bed. Maggie wasn't ready to confide in Lauren or forgive her completely so she dodged the question. She hadn't been mean to her but she was not going to give her what Lauren wanted on Lauren's timeframe. Besides the vortex of the betrayal had nothing to do with the night she had just lived with Paul.

I have to run, I'm meeting Weezie.

Wow, oh...oh...okay. See you, Maggie. I'll call when we get home.

Maggie turned from Lauren and headed toward the Backstage Cafe.

Chapter 54

Maggie pushed a cart. Weezie pushed a cart. They both stood in front of the homemade foods.
You know I think my salads look just as good as these.
Look what they charge for brownies.
Robbery.
They both looked at each other.
Are you getting a big idea like you did as a kid?
Not so big. But what if we made our own recipes and sold them next summer?
Oh my god. Maggie. It's a great idea. But let's try something the last week of this season.
Yes, let's. Meat loaf, ham salad, potato salad.
Maggie I just want you to know I'm not buying this food talk.
What?
You know what! You're making up a life and not telling me your real one.
What are you talking about? I heard Paul was around.
Yes.
And?
And he's going to Paris for three years.

Mary Keating

Oh, gosh, Maggie, I'm sorry. What happened?
Patrons wanted them there not in America. I just don't want to be torn up anymore. David and I getting divorced, Paul gone. I feel like right here; it will be good for me.
I hear ya. Okay back to food.
They moved their carts over to the bakery department.
You know Mom always wanted a picnic in the park.
Let's do it.
Quiche, Sangria, balloons.
They both echoed the dessert!
Brownies!

Chapter 55

A long picnic table was set up across from 33 James Avenue. Balloons adorned the trees. Friends and singers from the opera company mingled. Gretchen's grandchildren ran around.

Maggie called for everyone's attention with a clink of her glass. Weezie handed everyone a balloon.

I know Mom would love this. She loved this park.

Maggie began to choke up. Weezie took over.

So friends of Ann Michaels thank you all for coming. Let go your balloons and remember Ann.

The balloons rose into the cobalt sky beyond the maple trees.

Maggie noticed a car pull into the driveway. She left the celebration. Chris stepped out of the car.

Hi, Chris. Come on over. We're remembering my Mom.

Oh, no I just wanted to bring you a few papers to sign.

Sure.

Maggie stepped up to the porch.

David can have the house in Ithaca. No dogs, no children, we're pretty easy, aren't we?

Very straightforward if he agrees.

What do I have to do?
Nothing just sign these papers. I'll get in touch with David's lawyer and tell him you are starting divorce proceedings.
Chris handed her a pen. Maggie signed.
Okay, thanks. Now I need to get my car out I'm going off the grounds.
Is Lauren still here?
No she left.
Chris pulled out of the driveway. Maggie got into her car and drove to the Main Gate.
She showed her ticket and parking pass and drove away.
Maggie drove twenty minutes away to Westfield where the shores of Lake Erie began. The beach was filled with driftwood and stones. She remembered going to the beach when she was a child with her parents and Lauren. The beach wasn't crowded. She let the waves come up to her knees. They were wild today with the wind blowing hard. The waves: sh—wooshed in, sh—wooshed out. The beating sound washed away her divorce papers.
She called up Lauren's number. Lauren answered.
You made it home?
Oh, I forgot to call, sorry. What's up?
I'm here at Barcelona.
Really? We had fun as kids there on Sunday afternoons.
We did. I've met with Chris. I'm starting the divorce.
So much has happened Maggie, who could have known.
He asked about you.
Who?
Chris.

Chautauqua After Hours

Really?
Yeah.
Silence.
I'm staying at the house for awhile not going back to Ithaca.
Right.
Okay then, good-bye.
Good-bye and thanks Maggie.

Chapter 56

That night Maggie sat alone in a front row in the Amphitheater. Only street lamps reflected her thoughts. She began to hum. She wound her way up the steep ramp to the edge of the Amphitheater.

She wandered, distractedly, and found herself down the hill at the Bell Tower. It rang four times. Maggie looked up to see it was fifteen minutes past midnight. Here was one thing that never changed, she thought...the Bell Tower's ringing of time.

She took her shoes off and waded in the small ripples at the College Club beach. The moonbeams reached her feet.

Chapter 57

Two months later, on November first, Maggie and Weezie were busy cooking a brunch for a few 'foodies'. Maggie pulled out a tray of biscuits from the oven.
    She stopped cold. She stared at the biscuits. She heard Paul's voice.
    My Mamma makes the best biscuits in the state.
    She heard his words again. Louder.
    My Mamma makes the best biscuits in the state.
    Weezie noticed Maggie standing frozen in thought.
    What? Weezie asked.
    I'm going home.
    Now?
    Yep.
    Do I know what's happening?
    You do.
    God this is fantastic. As your best friend, I'm saying this is your *Eat, Pray, Love* moment.
    Do you think?
    Yep.
    Take me to the airport?
    I'll be right over, go pack.

Mary Keating

Maggie ran up the steps to the house. She turned the radio on. She threw her dresses and jeans in a suitcase.
She closed the bag and walked into the hall.
She phoned David and got his voice mail.
David you can send all the divorce papers to my box here and Weezie will pick them up. Take care, David.
Maggie took a last look around her Mother's bedroom. She walked down the stairs. She turned off the radio and locked the door.
Weezie waited outside in her Jeep. Maggie walked down the steps. She turned one last time to look at the house.
Maggie put her luggage in the back of the Jeep. She got in the passenger side. Weezie pulled away.
They reached the Buffalo airport in two hours. Maggie gave Weezie a hug before security.
You're no fool Maggie.
Hope not. David will send the divorce papers to my box.
Don't worry about him.
The whole house is empty now.
It will be here.
I have to run.
They embraced.
Send me a postcard from Paris.
Maggie waved and walked into the security line. She walked to the plane. On the plane she rested her head against a pillow. Southwest Airlines took off for New York City where she would get her connecting flight to Paris.

Chapter 58

After the long flight to Paris, Maggie taxied from the airport. She walked into a small hotel and climbed to the third floor to her small room. She collapsed on the bed.

The next evening she arrived at the theater looking lovely in pearls and a dress and heels. The show had not started. Someone told her there had been an accident backstage. Maggie hurried down a narrow hall.

She saw a crowd gathered around Paul Rains' stagedoor.

EMTs were lifting Paul onto a stretcher. Maggie pushed her way through the singers and crew. The EMTs placed the stretcher in the ambulance.

Maggie spun around looking for a familiar face.

She saw Evita who was weeping. Maggie leaned toward her.

Evita, do you remember me? Where are they taking Paul, what's happened? I'm Maggie from Chautauqua.

Evita couldn't concentrate.

I don't know, oh my god, it's Paul.

Maggie walked over to the officer.

Can you tell me what's happened? What hospital did they take him to? Hohs be tal? S'il vous plait?

Mary Keating

The American Hospital of Paris, it's about 6 kilometers away.
Maggie rushed outside to the curb. She hailed a taxi.
American Hospital of Paris please.
Oui, oui.
Maggie walked into the hospital. She asked at the front desk.
Paul Rains. Please, s'il vous plait. Paul Rains. They just brought him in.
The nurse looked puzzled by Maggie's response. She did not speak English.
Maggie screamed.
Does anyone speak English? Does anyone speak English?
Another nurse behind the desk answered.
Paul Rains is in room 308.
Maggie rushed to the elevator. She saw a doctor outside room 308.
Doctor can you tell me what's wrong with Paul?
She pointed to the door. He looked at her all out of breath. He spoke very fast with his French accent.
Your husband has Diabetes Type 2 and he is completely dehydrated which brought on the stroke.
Maggie gasped.
He's not my husband but we are ....are....
I'm afraid he needs to remain here for four or five days.
Yes, of course, thank you Doctor.

Chapter 59

Maggie roamed around in the beauty of Paris feeling numb. When she visited Paul the first few days he lay unconscious.

Four days later Maggie sat by Paul's bed. She placed her hand on his. He was awake.

Maggie, I can't believe you're here. Did I die?
You might have. It's Diabetes Type 2. Did you know?
I didn't. I just thought I was always thirsty.
Maggie squeezed his hand.
You're being discharged today.
Good, I want to show you something outside these walls.
Paul, do you know if you can go back on stage?
I'm not sure, they're very vague.

The orderly came to the door. He helped Paul into a wheelchair. He pushed him to the elevator. Maggie walked with him. They arrived at the first floor. Maggie followed the orderly to the front door.

Outside Paul tried to stand up. He sank into the wheelchair weak. Maggie thanked the orderly.

Merci.

She hailed a taxi. The taxi pulled up.

Will we go to your place, Paul?
No.
Maggie helped Paul into the taxi. The driver placed the wheelchair in the trunk.
Paul leaned on Maggie's shoulder.
Fontaine des Mers, s'il vous plait, asked Paul.
The taxi dropped them off at the end of the Champs Elysees. Paris looked beautiful in the blue hour.
Maggie walked alongside Paul as he wheeled himself to the Fontaine. Paul stopped the wheelchair and pulled the brake on.
Maggie oh, Maggie you came.
Maggie bent down and kissed Paul.
Paul took a French 'centime' and tossed it into the Fontaine des Mers. They looked at it for a long moment.
It reminds me of Chautauqua's fountain. I threw a penny in there the first day.
Maggie looked radiant.
Paul?
Yes?
Do you remember speaking about marriage? That last day at Chautauqua?
Maggie waited for him to say something. He remained silent. She hoped, now that she was there in Paris, he would really propose. When he quickly threw it out into the air of her Mother's home before he left she couldn't believe it. We could get married he had said. And what had she done? She ignored it hadn't she? Of course it was too much to put into any real thought for her life that quickly. Wasn't she in mourning? Didn't the cultural consensus tell everyone to wait

Chautauqua After Hours

a year before making any major decisions? Now after two months at the lake with the quiet and darkness of fall, chestnuts on the ground, maple leaves, crimson and orange and yellow, brisk winds of cold signaling winter creeping in she could finally feel this man.

He had just suffered a huge shock. He was not as well as Maggie thought when she first met him. And he had had no consciousness of his own body except his voice. Why did he always need to drink water? His throat and diaphragm were everything and now the rest of his body had gone berserk.

*****

Maggie looked and looked at the beauty of his head the head that sang like a lark here she was in the most romantic city on earth waiting wondering why she was wanting and what was the wonder and awe she thought she could see with the water shooting upward from the fountain all new sights and sounds foreign all language foreign the lights and love read about in every book heard in every song the Seine the Champs Elysees the Fontaine gushing up and here was Paul in a wheelchair spinning around and around ready to propose again she was sure of it oh yes she was a woman ready to say yes I will yes just like Molly Bloom in *Ulysses* it was going to be her moment

Paul finally spoke

Maggie I can't leave the tour

No of course not

No what I mean is I can't leave the tour because I can't

come back
    Maggie felt her scarf blow in the wind
    Maggie did you hear me
    A slight unraveling began in Maggie's mind a dread a loss of bearings though she knew she was in Paris her legs seemed weaker under her and the water in the Fontaine grew louder and she was sure there had been no proposal echoing through its liquid spray or her own desire
    Yes I heard you Paul then what am I doing here I guess this was a foolish mistake foolish to throw all caution to the wind as my Mother used to say I had it all wrong then didn't I
    No you didn't it was right in your Mother's home at Chautauqua we were going to be a new couple change our lives love in a new way it was all right then rising up out of Chautauqua and curtains and the piano and the dessert you served me but this sickness now it's unraveling my mind from my body suffering dialysis tubes needles blood work who knows what else and it's not good for you Maggie no I cannot give this to you and I cannot go back my Mamma knew it too when she said good bye I didn't know it
    I didn't know it either but I'm here with you and you'll get better
    I can't be a good man to you Maggie I'm nothing but a singer and now I will watch that go and see my voice get weaker and weaker becoming voiceless and I'll be out of the tour they won't keep me without a voice
    Maggie walked away from Paul's wheelchair
    He turned the wheelchair around and around he wheeled over to her

Chautauqua After Hours

Maggie you must go you must

Maggie turned toward him the shock of what she was hearing finally came through her heart other men might not ask her to leave they might hold on and depend on her to be the nurse and caretaker but Paul couldn't do it he was unselfish enough to sacrifice their love so that she would not be tied down in her 60s and beyond with medicinal needs and hospitals and doctors and gowns opening in the back and bedpans and needles and all the horror of sickness and dying

They were not married he had not proposed in Paris he was in a wheelchair already losing his strength not knowing how long before it would get much worse and she stood there with nothing to say

She bent down to his wheelchair so she could see his brown eyes once more look deep into the river of his soul and lay her head on his lap

She closed her eyes while a tear sneaked its way onto her cheek

He laid his hand on her head

I am nothing but this big body all heavy body of sickness and my voice my voice will go Maggie and I can't bear that day for me or for us please don't hold on

*****

The airplane ride was silent and Maggie was grateful she wanted to feel her feet on the earth before she could make sense of the last week of her life she landed at the Buffalo airport and rented a car her entire existence locked into the driving home to Chautauqua while her subconscious threw darts at her and her conscious mind raged at her for not staying and changing his mind while her cosmic sense of life kicked in and she saw it as fate and then what did all of it mean really the flirting and getting to know another man after years of marriage now her life was suspended behind the wheel unable to turn the music on as she sped down the road to exit 60 toward Westfield the town where she had watched her Mother die just four and a half months earlier now she was speeding back to Chautauqua by herself living with all her cells pulsating down the last stretch of road on her Aboriginal 'walkabout' she knew every tree and farmhouse down the road through the small town of Mayville past the Lighthouse grocery store to the main gate and through the gate she drove relieved it was not summer there was no attendant and no need to buy a gate ticket she drove along Massey to James Avenue where she heard herself crying

I have to make it

I have to make it

As if she were afraid if she stopped saying this mantra the heavens would open up and Chautauqua would disappear swallowed up lost forever and if Chautauqua was lost forever then she would be lost forever she hadn't always been conscious of that knowledge but now she knew that she belonged to Chautauqua because her Mother belonged to Chautauqua and if she didn't remember this fact by thinking back through her Mother's life she would forget and fall into utter chaos again and again and the thought of that was nothing she could endure again she was sixty time to understand her life time to bring the threads together in one big quilt time to get home and climb the stairs to her Mother's bedroom time to look out

Chautauqua After Hours

the window to the park time to feel the pulses and rhythms of the house because time itself would live there with the paint on the walls and the food in the refrigerator and the glads on the porch and the china tea cups that she would sip her tea from with her own song of eternity embracing her time to know every memory every photograph every summer on the red-brick walk every moment of love unspoken between them time to hear the tides of her blood beating back through her Mother's heart and time to listen to the haunting whispers of Chautauqua

Yes it was true she was awake now...

Thinking of it all as she opened the front door...

It was this house that her heart would beat on for...

Here at Chautauqua the place she loved more than any other...

She couldn't give it up...

Not now not ever...

Separation was impossible...

AND the Bell Tower could be heard...

...GONG

...GONG

...GONG...

CPSIA information can be obtained
at www.ICGtesting.com
Printed in the USA
BVHW082247040619
550189BV00001BA/20/P